Cold Suspenders

by

Alvin Finch

**Grosvenor House
Publishing Limited**

Alvin Finch is hereby identified as author of this
work in accordance with Section 77 of the Copyright, Designs
and Patents Act 1988

The book cover picture is copyright to Alvin Finch

This book is published by
Grosvenor House Publishing Ltd
28-30 High Street, Guildford, Surrey, GU1 3HY.
www.grosvenorhousepublishing.co.uk

A CIP record for this book
is available from the British Library

ISBN 978-1-906210-89-2

Cold Suspenders

I

In Suspense

Morton wriggled his toes, then his fingers. He relaxed for a moment: then began to reach in his mind for his knees and elbows. He had performed this routine many times before. As he built up the image of his limbs moving, he realised that maybe he hadn't wriggled his toes. He concentrated for what seemed an eternity on opening his eyes. Eventually his left eye opened. The compartment he was in was barely visible. This puzzled him. Normally when he regained consciousness all of his faculties returned reasonably quickly.

The compartment Morton was in was one of two hundred reserved for senior employees of the James Pescold Foundation. Each of the compartments was designed to place a human body in cryogenic suspension. Morton had entered the compartment for a routine balancing exercise. The object of which was twofold, the blood proxy machine was able to recalibrate itself to his current body state, and the occupiers were able to accustom themselves to the procedure. This procedure had been instituted after several disasters, when people reawakening from suspension panicked causing severe heart strain. The chemical balance of the proxy blood has to be exactly right. In particular too little diotric will cause the patient's organs to crack up. Too much and the body is unable to clear it from the system. In most cases a full blood flush is not done. In fact this is a very risky business as diotric is designed with a decay period.

Morton mused to himself that maybe the machine had for some reason replaced his blood with proxy. He could not understand how this could be as he was very particular in tending to his own machine. In fact he was very worried. His capsule was set up to perform a full cryo operation, and he only ever entered if for relaxation and calibration purposes. The dioric/decay mixture was set for full strength with 50 years decay built in. As his eyesight cleared he racked his brains trying to recall if he had upset any of the parameters before he entered the cell. He also tried to think strong relaxing thoughts. He realised that if he had been administered proxy, his life was hanging in the balance.

The display film in front of him gradually became visible. As it did so he recognised that a full cryo cycle must have been instigated. He realised that the letters on the display paper had been slowly changing due to the low temperature, confusing his eyesight. The display was now indicating a temperature just above the freezing point of water. He was at the same time very worried, and relieved. Worried that a full cycle had taken place, and relieved that at least his brain had not turned to mush. The fact that his brain was working probably meant that the rest of his body was in good shape.

Waiting for the temperature to increase he recalled the events of the previous day. He had been involved in several discussions and near arguments on the future of the company. In common with the other founding scientists he found himself increasingly annoyed with the accountants banging on about shareholders and profits. The Foundation was originally set up to be a non-profit making research organisation. As time went on more and more of its inventions had been licensed to profit making organisations. The profit from this was originally all ploughed back into research. All of the original employees of the company owned shares. As the years went by and people moved on or retired, these shares had gradually made their way into the open market. The holders of these shares were now demanding bigger and bigger dividends, pointing to the huge profits that the company made. Morton had never sold any of his shares and was now the biggest single shareholder in the company. This often enabled him to block the things he didn't like, as his colleagues would vote with him. He could not see why the company should be paying out large sums of money to strangers when the company had a huge number of employees to support.

The original ethos of the company had been to have all of an employee's basic needs supplied by the company. In addition to this, employees were given a small salary, and if the company did well, and was able to make money out of some research, a share dividend would be issued, often more than adequately supplementing the salary. From the start the company realised that non-scientists as well as scientists were needed, and provided cross training. The aim had been that any employee could take any career progression they liked through the company, which now owned several training organisations. These businesses provided training to the Foundation employees, and sold spare capacity on the open market. Employees were able to reasonably easily transfer between companies.

Morton had always been against personnel being able to sell their shares on the open market, but in a test case taken to the World Court of Humane Justice a Judge had ruled that they must behave as other companies. After that there was a flurry of share selling from the retired members. An association of Pescold shareholders had been formed. Morton felt that the only aim of this association was to run a business to mess with the Pescold business. Morton hated this and was forever locked in combat with members of the association.

II

Suspended

At this point perhaps we should look back at what had happened some time earlier, where we find Paul Barton and Morton in the cryogenic lab.

Paul Barton had checked over Morton Elise's compartment several times before. He had often helped Morton do his personal overhaul. In return Morton would check out Paul's pod for him. The ever-present danger of nuclear war (after the New Republic of Pacifica crisis) had sparked the building of the compartments. The company had originally envisaged the most senior research engineers and administrators using the pods to wait for the surrounding radioactivity to subside. The survivors could then hopefully rebuild some of what had been created. Drugs to help stave off the effects of radioactivity had been created, but after the ban on any animal testing the company had been unable to verify the effectiveness of the drugs. The rest of the foundation had been issued with survival packs containing amongst other things these drugs.

The chamber that Paul was now leaning over was one of the products of the foundation's research teams. The chamber could be used in slightly different ways. A human body could be administered a small quantity of drugs and then chilled. Those rich people who can afford to spend vast sums on prolonging their lives of course use the chilling process. As a body does not age while in this state a person can enter the capsule for a period of sleep and not get any older. This state can usually be maintained only for periods of hours or at most a day. The drug diotric is required in large doses to enable longer periods of suspension to be undertaken. The machine removes most of a person's blood, and replaces if with a chemical solution. The balance of chemicals in the solution must be precise.

Paul was supposedly helping Morton to calibrate his capsule to his current body state. The presence of the cryogenic chambers was kept a tight secret. Paul was the only non-foundation member that knew of their existence. Paul was a member of the Pescold Association and owned a large number of shares. He was superficially very friendly with Morton, but was starting to secretly harbour a personal and professional dislike for him. At the current moment he was engaging himself in freezing Morton's body for the next few hundred years. With Morton's influence gone he could sway company matters his own way, and follow various devious plans he had cooked up with some other associates.

This was the culmination of a Plan that Paul had hatched some time ago. It had taken him a long time to persuade the foundation to institute various security measures. These had been helped along by a terrorist attack on one of the buildings. In actual fact Paul had provided the terrorist organisation with plans of the building that was attacked. Electronic cards were now issued to all personnel, and the 'home' locations of employees kept secret.

Pescold was of course one of the first companies to take up the use of Hooks. The great majority of employees now worked from Home Office Outpost Key Services sites, or from home. Paul had first met Morton when the Foundation was initially considering using Hooks. They had spent many hours together thrashing out what staff and services were required in a Hook. Of course we all take Hooks for granted nowadays, and it is hard to imagine the hoards of people that used to travel several kilometres to work either by themselves or in incredibly cramped conditions. One might complain sometimes that the Hook that one is using is cramped on a busy day, forgetting the horrible inconveniences of days gone by.

It is not widely known that Paul Barton was one of the Hook pioneers. Paul had always kept a low profile in meetings, preferring to hatch schemes in private. Many people thought that he was an estate agent. In the early days of Hooks Paul liked to meet the customers and determine himself what their general needs were. The talks with Morton had enabled Paul to gain an insight into the workings of the foundation, and to use some of their inventions in his setting up of Hooks. In fact it was Paul Barton who saw the potential for using a combination of SoundBarrier and ElectroBrella to create the al fresco office. During a chat with Morton about Beethoven's Pastoral Symphony the conversation had strayed into hi-fi systems and Electro-static interference. They then hit on the idea of making use of the unavoidable 'hum' created by the ElectroBrella. By changing the noise produced to a sound counteracting the background noise, the weather-proof soundproof outdoor office was created. Of course, and as we know, the authorities still cannot agree if this comprises an enclosed space as far as smoking is concerned.

The public Hooks security, as we know has its faults, but it is reasonably reliable. As you may know various security schemes have been tried, but eventually it was decided that the old-fashioned International ID card was as good as any scheme. Retinal and hand scanning machines had been tried but produced a spate of people having their hands and eyeballs removed. The security at the Foundation's central site was originally non-existent, as it was easy to recognise an intruder. With the advent of Hooks of course people had less need to visit the main site. The company also grew larger once free of building space constraints. The security at the main site requires an ID card to gain entry to the main building. A receptionist then may check your details further if you are not recognised. After some procrastination Morton agreed to this, as he could keep his ID card in his pocket and walk about the building unchallenged. Gradually a monitoring system had been build into the system that logs where in the building someone is. Morton had also originally objected to this. After a pilot system had been installed Morton found it useful to locate his co-workers, and had acquiesced.

As we have discussed previously this was all in Paul's plan. He had entered the building with Morton and gone with him to the chambers located underneath the controlled substances storage area. The logging system of course had recorded their access to the room.

Paul stood to one side while Morton entered the capsule. Morton rippled his fingers across the DynoPin plate, and checked the results on the display paper. Morton had refitted his capsule a year or so before. He had replaced the old-fashioned keyboard and LCD display with a DynoPad and Display paper. He had promised to refit Paul's chamber as the improvements make it much easier to enter the capsule. Paul chatted to him about this as Morton settled himself into the pod. As Morton lowered the lid, Paul curled his fingers around the edge of the door and depressed the full Cryo button. Morton was totally unaware of this and continued chatting to Paul not noticing the warning message etching itself on the Display Paper. If it had been fitted with the current advances in Display Paper, Morton might have noticed a colour change. When the lid finally clicked shut Barton checked that the active light was lit. He took some Blu-Tack from his pocket and carefully rolled it into a sphere. The normally dull blue indicator light outside the pod was now vivid red. The light was in a slight recess, and it was into the recess that Paul dropped the blue sphere. Stepping back he checked his handiwork. The Blu-Tack ball looked exactly like the light on an inactive pod. All Paul had to do now was to make it look as though both of them had left the building.

Part of this plan was easy. He had made sure that Morton's ID card was in the pocket of his jacket, which had been carelessly discarded over some equipment. He picked up the jacket and headed for the exit. The controlled substances room has a system that ensures that persons are counted in and out. There are two doors close together which ensure that only one person at a time can enter and leave. The outer door has a letterbox gap in it to allow staff to pass small items in and out. Paul opened the first door and allowed it to close behind him. He pushed on the outer door and heard the door behind him click locked. He made his exit and turned round.

He had with him a folding umbrella, which had caused Morton some amusement, as the weather had been fine for several days. He extended the umbrella to its full length and inserted into the letterbox slot. He pushed on the inner door and opened it. The furled umbrella being a thin item did not trigger the body detector. He pulled the umbrella away from the inner door and unfurled it at the same time, thus fooling the sensors into believing that a person had entered the gap. He pulled the umbrella forward and heard the rear door click.

He then opened the outer door and retrieved the umbrella.

Hanging Morton's jacket on the end of the umbrella and placing it over his shoulder he then walked though the building and down to the reception area. As he passed sensors in the building they detected two people walking one behind the other. The recording cameras picked up the rather strange sight of Paul with umbrella and trailing jacket. This did not over-concern Paul. By the time anyone might suspect anything the recording discs would be overwritten by a following week's data. Before entering the reception area he removed the jacket from the umbrella, folded up the umbrella and placed it in the inside pocket of the jacket.

The girl at the reception desk was sitting reading a book on the application of wave dynamics in sub-karpovion gravity situations. The girl was a recent graduate and had joined the foundation to further study the application of reverse gravity effects. Paul stopped at the desk. He leant on the desk and spoke to the girl. "Hello Katei," he said. "How's the studies?" She stopped reading and looked at Paul. She was not at all sure about him, and thought of him as a sort of toad hopping about. She had seen him and Morton go into the building earlier, and looked behind him to see if Morton was on his way. Morton, she thought, she rather liked. He was, maybe, about fifteen years older than her, she thought, but she was nevertheless rather taken by him.

In Katei 's opinion the suits that Paul Barton wore were too 'sharp'. On the other hand, she mused Morton, was never really that well dressed. Something that she was sure she could do something about. Getting him dressed up a bit better.

Paul Barton was glad to make a quick exit from the building, as he did not like the look that the girl at the desk had given him. He felt that she had been looking at him like some sort of slimy creature. Barton, otherwise felt quite well. It was a sunny day, and the pollen count was low. The bad sneezes that hurt his head would not trouble him that day, and neither would Morton. Paul tried to shut out the nagging voices of uncertainty in his head.

III

Suspenders

A few weeks before the aforementioned activity took place between Paul and Morton the company had funded a beano in celebration of the release of a new electric shaver, the DiShave. The shaver gently pulls on a hair, bleaches, and cuts. The shaver was expected to sell well to both men and women. For men, five o'clock shadow would now be a thing of the past.

Morton had returned to the bar to collect a martini, having been wearied by a discussion on ingrown hairs and the precision of the new shaver. Being a reasonably senior employee, and also a bit older, other colleagues would often seek his approbation. He tipped the remains of the beer down his throat, and gladly accepted the martini from the barman. As he turned from the bar he nearly collided with a young lady behind him. They both began to apologise to each other, in the way one does if you are not sure whose fault it is. Having got the apologies over with they both felt impromptu introductions were in order.

In fact the introductions were one way, as Katei knew all about Morton. Morton had to rack his brains for a few seconds. He remembered seeing her CV the previous year when a batch of graduate applications had arrived. He had spent a bit longer on her CV than others. His interest had not been so much due to the academic content, more with the attached hologram. He had taken an immediate liking to her appearance, and was further struck by the picture, which showed her suspended in mid air. He had wondered how the hologram had got through vetting procedures. Pictures of candidates had to be original, and not altered in any way. This was what reminded him that her subject was gravity, or more exactly, anything that allowed one to escape it. The picture backed up her CV by showing her using a karpovion gravity 'anti' wave effect.

They chatted firstly about work subjects. Initially Morton was worried that she might continue in the same vein as the boorish fellow he had just thrown off. After about five minutes the conversation changed to cycling. This was a result of talking about gravity waves, and friction reducing devices. It turned out that they both owned bikes for pleasure as well as using public bikes. Katei lamented the fact that while she was working at the main building she could only visit the countryside at weekends. The company owns dormitory units within cycling distance of its buildings, and expects employees and families to use them rather than spend huge sums on daily commuting.

Katei was immensely pleased that Morton was spending so long talking to her. Morton found Katei very pleasant, maybe too pleasant. Morton was about 38 perhaps; though he looked younger due to spending a lot of nights in the CryoCapsule which he had made use of for at least the last 10 years. He mused that Katei must be about 22, just old, or young, enough to be his daughter. He found himself agreeing with her to go for a quick drink at a local pub, followed by something to eat.

While they had been speaking the party had been gradually coming to an end. They made their way to the exit collecting their outdoor capes on the way. Morton would have been much happier with his old-fashioned overcoat, but as far as he could determine no one made any reasonably priced ones any more, and he didn't want to wear out the only one he had. He hoped that one day fashions would change again. The cape he believed was a creation of marketing. The material that a modern day cape is made out of, although being waterproof yet breathing does not easily lend itself to the cutting and welding or stitching that is required for pockets. When they emerged outside he was glad of the over-garment, as the evening was cold and wet.

They walked to the Pug and Parrot in the steady drizzle, discussing what and where they would eat. Katei was a fan of Afrikaans cooking. Morton was of the opinion that the food tasted too greasy. Eventually they settled on a Norman restaurant that both of them had been meaning to try. Soft rain had come after a couple of hot days, and the smells released by the gentle precipitation reminded them both of separate visits to the north of the continent.

The pub was particularly pleasantly warm, and as they sipped their drinks Morton tried not to examine Katei's cleavage too closely. He felt decidedly uneasy. It had been a long time since he had last been out with a woman in a pleasure situation. Katei on the other hand was feeling quite ebullient. When she visited the washroom she had given her bra a couple of clicks to accentuate her cleavage. This is what had set off Morton's uneasiness. As they talked Katei deliberately made lots of eye contact, and placed her hands near his on the table.

They finished their drinks in a leisurely fashion. Downing the last couple of drops they nodded farewell to the barman and headed for the restaurant. The restaurant was within 10 minutes walk of the Pug and Parrot, which was one of the swaying factors in choosing it. The menu was not particularly extensive, but the place was well known for fresh food and interesting 'Specials of the Day'. They briefly sat down with a martini each, perusing the menu and examining the specials blackboard. They were then ushered to their table, by a very obliging waiter.

Nothing much was said during the meal as the food required almost all of their attention. The conversation resumed properly after the desert had been consumed and calvados served. Morton brought up the subject of Katei's photograph in her application. Normally Morton disliked discussing work outside of working hours, but he found Katei's description of her researches interesting. As they came toward the end of the calvados Katei suggested that perhaps Morton might like to come back to her apartment and see some of the experiments that she had created at home. Morton was by now slightly squiffy anyway, and agreed with no hesitation. They already had a taxi on the way as the waiter had pointed out that the rain was now very heavy.

As they got out of the taxi and stood in the porch outside Katei's rooms Morton remarked on the size of the apartment. He had assumed that as she had been doing some researches at home that she would have a larger apartment. Katei giggled at this and said, "No need, I do most of my researches in bed."

The size of the apartment was in fact quite deceptive, as the rooms extended into two levels of basement, as well as the ground floor.

Morton settled himself into a chair and Katei poured a couple of drinks, and put the coffee machine into motion. "Right," she said, "I think it's time for me to get on the bed and show you my suspenders." Morton reacted to this by spluttering a mouthful of drink over his arm and the arm of the chair. She retired into the bedroom unzipping her garments as she went. Morton didn't know whether to be excited or worried.

Katei appeared five minutes later rather scantily clad in a material that had a metallic sheen. "Come on," she said to Morton, "I just want to show you how my suspenders work". Morton tried to stop his face going red but to no avail. "It's a gravity suspense suit," she explained, "designed to enhance a body's susceptibility to anti-gravity". She led Morton into the bedroom.

There were a few small plastic boxes plugged together with no obvious function. Four larger boxes appeared to be non-potential energy collectors. Morton had read about these, but had not fully come to grips with the physics behind them. As he understood it the 'Nonpots' collected unused gravitational and magnetic potential energy. He asked Katei about them. "My suspenders," she said. "I use these devices to create a kind of non gravity effect," she explained. As she spoke she moved forward and moved as if to lie on the bed. She ended up suspended above the bed. "Try pushing me," she said to Morton. He tried and was surprised when she shot over the other side of the room. "Whoops," she giggled, "you don't know your own strength." Morton found this quite fascinating.

Katei pointed to a cupboard at the end of the bed. "There's another suit in there". Morton opened the cupboard and removed the suit. "Go on," laughed Katei, "put it on." Morton in his excitement (and possibly squiffy state) forgot all modesty and removed his clothes to don the suit. If Katei had not been suspended she might have fallen over. Having donned the suit he moved forward to where Katei was, beginning to float as he did so. "Well," remarked Katei, "I've got you into bed then," and started laughing again. Morton went red again and started to stutter. "Never mind" said Katei "I'll tell people we were just experimenting." Katei thought to herself that there was some more experimenting that she would like to do. Especially after have just seen Morton undress.

Katei explained some of the gravitational effects to Morton as they floated about inside the bubble. She explained that Newton mechanics appeared to be altered. Normal action and reaction did not take place, for example. She explained in some depth about her analysis of loop quantum gravity, and the effects of quantum mechanical spin. Morton lay floating for a while listening to the pretty girl talking to him. He wished that he were slightly younger, as he felt himself more attracted to her, and the depth of her knowledge fascinated him.

Morton retired to the bathroom to replace his clothes in a somewhat more decorous fashion than he had removed them. They moved back out to the living room and finished their drinks. Morton thanked her for the education and bade her goodnight to return to his foundation-provided rooms.

IV

Out of Suspense

We now return to where we left off earlier in this narration. Morton had been gently dreaming of humid summer air, good food, wine and company. As he awakened, he realised that his limbs felt very stiff.

Morton realised that he must have temporarily slipped into unconscious as the capsule was now brightly lit, and his sense of touch was returning. He started to gently move his fingers and toes. To his great relief his body appeared to be responding, albeit slowly, to his brain's commands. The DynoPin plate was resting under Morton's hand. He summoned up the energy to create the finger movements required to control the display output. He wanted to see what time it was. The readout confused him. It looked like he had been under for a couple of hours, but the day of the week was wrong. He thought that perhaps several days had passed. He was greatly confused by the year displayed. It looked like he had gone back about 50 years to the mid nineteen hundreds. He knew that the capsule was an advanced bit of equipment, but not so advanced that he could travel backward in time. As he mused on this he became aware that a red warning light had lit. The screen in front of him cleared and two messages were displayed:

```
panic — task scheduler, sleeping child has run time
backward
System RB_PANIC system going down in 01 minutes.
```

Morton had some experience with computers and realised that the computer running his life support systems was about to restart. There were in actual fact several computers in the system, but he was worried that if the master machine restarted, the others might follow suit, and cause a hiccup in his waking process. He quickly entered a key sequence that gave him access to the operating system. Once inside the system he then disabled the program that was about to shut the system down. He breathed a slight sigh of relief, but was still concerned that the system was now not functioning correctly.

Morton could hear an alarm sounding. The sound was somewhat muffled by the capsule's insulation, but he decided that it was probably loud enough to summon help. As he waited for help to arrive he amused himself by looking for the cause of the computer problem. His fingers gently undulated over the computer pad as he examined the system.

Katei Cooksie was spending the weekend at work, catching up on some of her private projects. She was investigating several aspects of magnetism that had parallels with her gravity work. She had for some time now been investigating the possibility of another force. Several people had tried to tie together electricity, magnetism and gravity. Katei had decided, from her gravity research, that each of these forces was separate, and that the 'other' force provided the mechanism for these to interact. She was using the foundation's computer systems to model various equations that she had devised. Normally she would be able to access the network from home, but the particular computer system she was using contained sensitive data and was not attached to the general network.

She had started a set of calculations running and had sat back to think. As she did so she could hear an alarm of some sort in the distance. As far as she was aware there were only two people in the building, and she could see the other person behind a glass partition. Katei picked up another computer pad, and signed on as a building co-ordinator. After a few finger movements she discovered that the alarm was coming from the controlled substances room. She brought up the room access log, only to discover that no-one had entered the room that weekend. The fault, she decided, must be some kind of computer network failure. Moving her fingers a bit more revealed that several computers were reporting re-starts for no apparent reason. An item that further interested her was that the machines appeared to be in a secure area.

After some further finger work on the keyboard she discovered that the failing machines were unable to synchronise their clocks with the network, each machine was complaining about a date fault. Katei suddenly realised that these were computers with operating systems that had not been made properly year 2000 compliant. As far as she knew all of the computers in the establishment had recently been verified for date compliance. Some of the so-called Y2K fixes had only extended the clock life of an operating system for about twenty years, and some for maybe as little as ten. She realised that wherever these secure machines were, no one had noticed them.

She looked over at the other person in the building. They appeared so totally engrossed in their work that they had not noticed the alarm. Katei decided that she would investigate the malfunction herself – it would give her something to do while her equations were being processed.

She had recently acquired very senior status at the foundation, and was able to enter the controlled substances room. She was one of only six people who had this access. Four of these were very senior staff, and the other two the founders, Barton and Elise. As far as she knew no one had heard much from Barton for about six years, and Morton had become a recluse about eight years ago. She thought about Morton for a bit, remembering his eagerness to try out her equipment, and his embarrassment when he realised that he was naked. They had both been a bit under the influence, she decided.

After going through the entry performance to the controlled substance area Katei stood and looked about her. She was reasonably sure that all of the machines in this area had been certified, upgraded, or replaced. It then occurred to her that she should check the Cryo Room, this having probably been left out of the audit process. This room was the sole preserve of the founders. She wondered for a moment if she should try and get a message to one of them. After a moment's hesitation she decided not. She had several times tried to contact

Morton, but had only got stiff, almost computer speak replies. Barton she utterly disliked.

Everything in the Cryo room looked normal. There was of course no reason why it should not. A lot of boxes and equipment, some with lights, some without.

She cast her eyes over the capsules. All of them apart from one had flashing blue lights. She turned around and was surprised to see that the master console was an old-fashioned Cathode Ray Tube device. She thought all of these had been scrapped near the start of the century. The console showed that all of the systems were constantly re-starting, apart from one. She decided that the best thing would be to isolate the systems from the rest of the network until a technician could be found to correct the problems. The system being somewhat out of date she was not sure how to do this. In fact she was interested that the system was still compatible with the rest of the network. It then occurred to her that the system must be physically wired into the 'old' network, which would contain protocol converters. She located a socket in the wall and removed a plug. After about ten minutes error messages stopped flooding the main console, and the systems appeared to have stabilised.

She cast her eyes over the capsules again. All of them now showed green lights apart from one that was a dull blue. This intrigued her and she decided to investigate. As she got closer, she realised that something was lodged in the recess that contained the indicator light. She took her pen out of her pocket and used it to flick the offending item out of the hole. She could now see that a light was glowing red. Emblazoned on the door of the capsule was a message: 'If red light shows, the capsule is active, DO NOT ENTER'. She decided that no one could possibly be in one of these capsules, and that there must be a malfunction of some description.

The door opened with a touch of stiffness, and she peered inside. What she saw made her let out a scream. At least she thought she screamed, it might have been a whimper. A green creature was occupying the pod. She stood unable to move, with her eyes fixed on this creature. The lips of the creature moved slightly, and then it started to lick its lips. The thought that it might eat her went through her mind. Gradually she managed to get a hold of herself and think straight. She realised that the creature was speaking in a whisper. She leant forward to listen. "Flush button," it said. At the same time its fingers wiggled. About six inches away from the end of its fingers was a small button marked Diotric flush. She pressed the button, and then took another more careful look at the creature. It was a human, and not really that green. In fact any greenness was fast disappearing. Katei felt faint for a moment; she suddenly realised that this was one of the few men that she had seen naked (as he was in the pod). She was looking at Morton, but a Morton who must be much closer to her own age.

Morton meanwhile was thanking his maker for the unexpected intrusion. The system that should have started the flushing must have been one of the computer tasks that had failed. In his weak state he was unable to reach the button to do it manually. He decided that a bit of re-design was in order. After about ten minutes he tried a tentative throat-clearing cough. This made Katei jump. She had been standing waiting for something to happen.

"Don't I know you from somewhere?" Morton asked. "Yes," squeaked Katei, who was trying to work out what was going on. "I am not sure," he said, "but you look like you might be Katei's older sister, or something." "No," she replied, "it's me." As she said this it sounded stupid to her. She tried to explain herself but got her words even further tangled up. Eventually Morton cut in. "What date is it? What year is it?" On hearing Katei's answer he uttered the word "Shit!" then he asked, "Where's Paul? Paul Barton?" She replied that she had not seen him for a few years, and that she thought that they had both deliberately hidden themselves.

During the following conversation Morton was able to explain that any voice or e-mail sent to him was probably being auto answered, as his mailbox must be full. Katei asked how his shares had been so well managed in the past few years. He replied that this was also a computer-automated process mostly linked to the Foundation computers. "That would explain why you have not done so much for the past year then," said Katei. "How?" asked Morton. "Your network link to the Foundation was removed," she replied, "Barton supplied the authority to do it." She went on, "All of the world has been wondering how a billionaire like yourself" should suddenly slow up his trading". "Billionaire?" ejected Morton. "Yes," Katei answered.

V

Back Into the World

Katei and Morton talked for some time, speculating on how Morton had become trapped in the capsule. They eventually came to the (as we know, correct) conclusion that Paul Barton wanted Morton out of the way. Morton would not believe that Paul would try to kill him, but Katei persuaded him otherwise. The building in which the pods were housed was due to be closed down the following year, and sold for re-building. Paul had been instrumental in deciding the move from the current building to another. Part of the process of moving would have been to de-commission all of the equipment. As very few knew much about the room they were in, it would be more than likely that Morton would have only been discovered after the machines had been turned off. His death would then have been put down to a tragic accident.

Morton decided that he would remain a 'hermit' for some time longer until he could work out what Paul Barton was up to. As far as Morton could work out from what Katei had told him, Paul had been re-structuring the Foundation in such a way that large parts of it could be sold off. Part of this process was what had created the large dividends that Morton's computer had re-invested. Dividends that Paul Barton must have also raked off himself.

The immediate problem was to leave the room they were in without setting off any alarms. Katei had been trying to work out how the two of them were going to get out of the room, as only one had been counted in. Morton regarded Katei for a moment or two, and then the doorway. "Well," Morton said, "you are quite slim, and I am not that fat. I think we could probably squeeze through the connecting doors together." "Mmm," replied Katei, "I would say that you only poke out in very appropriate areas," It was at this point that Morton realised that he had been happily chatting to Katei while being stark naked. As he started to go red Katei tried to reassure him that she wasn't in the least worried by this. After a brief bit of scurrying around she managed to retrieve his clothes for him, minus his jacket containing his ID card of course. This lack of ID was discovered after a thorough search of the lab.

Katei pointed out that Morton would be restricted in movement without an ID card. Morton pulled a funny face and said, "No problem I think." "How come?" asked Katei. "We have some, 'special' ID cards in here." he replied. He went on to explain that Paul had thought it a good idea to 'invent' some people. "But how?" enquired Katei. "I thought the ID system was foolproof?" Morton went on to explain that the foundation had had a hand in the development of the system. One of the requirements that the government had specified was that an ID could be fabricated by the security services, both for use by the security services and for providing 'cover' to people who had turned informer on major crimes. He further explained that Paul had thought it a good idea for those people in the pods to be able to re-emerge and blend into whatever the current society might be. Assuming of course that the ID card system was still working.

Morton struggled into his clothes, and then crossed the room to where a safe was let into the wall. He had to have two goes at unlocking the safe as his voice was a bit creaky, and the safe failed to recognise him the first time. The safe intrigued Katei. She asked Morton how it worked. Morton explained that it was a project that never took off properly. When he had spoken to the safe he had said, "Sometimes the rain can be bad and one would like to be in Spain, and not on the Falls road. But mainly, on the whole, the opportunities are quite plain." The safe, he expanded, was voice and word activated and needed a certain sequence of words with separating words. "This phrase was obvious of course. The rain in Spain falls mainly on the plain." He also explained how the safe could detect stress in a persons voice (for instance if the owner was being forced to open it) and refuse to open. "But what if someone overhears you?" asked Katei. "They could also then open the safe." "Well," said Morton, "you just have to be a bit careful with your core words, and always put lots of other words round them. The same phrase will not work twice. Anyway the safe didn't catch on because people found it too complex to use. But I am sure it just needed a bit more thinking about"

He reached inside the safe and extracted a blank ID card and large black box. "Right," he said, "who am I going to be?"

They both could think of easy names such as Fred Bloggs, Mickey Mouse and Ford Prefect. They spent a quarter of an hour or so until they came up with the name Virgil Tracy. Katei was sure that someone famous had been called that, but Morton said it had just popped into his head, and sounded like a good name. He suggested that perhaps she was thinking of the author Virgil. Morton pulled the fibre optic cable out of the back of the black box and plugged it into the computer pad that he always kept in his pocket. After a few minutes of keying away he declared, "There! All done; Meet Mister Tracy!" "Pleased to meet you," answered Katei. "Now can we get out of here?"

"Hold on a minute Missus Tracy I've got something to tidy up," replied Morton. "Missus Tracy?" queried Katei; "Yes," responded Morton, "I thought that it would be handy if you also has another persona."

Morton put the black box back in the safe, and replaced the cover of the Cryo Capsule. When this had been done they squeezed together in the exit chamber. Morton had placed the ID cards in a special pocket that stopped the cards transmitting their presence to the system. The pocket had originally been designed to stop radiation from a mobile phone reaching inside a body. Morton had wrapped the pocket right around the cards. When they emerged into the main corridor Morton was struck by the shabbiness of the building. "This stuff shouldn't wear out for years," he remarked to Katei. "Yes, but it's been years since it was all put in," she replied, "and anyway money is very tight. Better that the money is spent on research rather than posh environment." Morton agreed with her a to a certain extent, but still felt that the surrounds could be a lot nicer. "Is this Paul's doing then?" he asked. "I suppose it is," replied Katei. "Everyone is worried that if he goes on insisting cutting budgets and staff that there will soon be no one left to earn the Foundation money."

Morton explained to Katei his plan for leaving the building. He would go out first carrying all of the IDs, the two new ones in his secure pocket. He would then return to the building with Katei's ID in his pocket and the new ones out. Katei would let him in as two visitors and they would then leave together

As it was a weekend the reception area was empty and they hoped to carry out the plan without any hitches. This proved true and they were soon on their way to the railway station via Katei's house (to collect a change of clothing for her). One or two people gave Morton odd looks on the way, as his clothing style was somewhat out of date. Morton's attire had always been a bit unusual anyway, and he did not notice the glances he was given. Katei had noticed, and remarked on this to Morton. "The only thing that doesn't look out of place is your overcoat," she opined. "It used to be the thing that everyone thought unusual," he replied. "It's just as well that I am not wearing the jacket I had with me, as it was considered trendy at the time."

It took a while to get to the railway station, and when they reached it Morton wandered around the building looking for a timetable. "Blasted stupid, this," he exploded to Katei, "I would have thought that someone would be able to produce a simple timetable by now!" Katei had a look at the timetable and then back at Morton. "No problem with this," she said, "it's a Shuttle cum Express station."

"A what?" queried Morton. "Ah!" she ejected, "of course you wouldn't know about this. About six years ago they started introducing driver-less trains that shuttle from one station to the next. On this line where there are about fifteen stations between town and country there are about twenty driver-less coaches. The timetable you read shows what positioning algorithm is used, so that you can get an idea of when a coach will be available. Of course most people don't understand it, and some of the coaches are reserved for freight."

As she spoke the public announcement system burst into life. "Stand back! Stand back! Behind the Yellow Line please," they were commanded. A carriage hurtled into view, slowed as it passed through the station and then sped off again. "Nothing new then," declared Morton. Katei looked at the timetable again. "Express on the way," she explained. "When a limited stop express train is due the other carriages shuffle themselves to the other end of the track or to the nearest siding. Of course in the early days there were not enough sidings as the track company had sold off adjoining land and had to buy new land for sidings."

A multi-coach train now came into view. Morton was puzzled by the fact that the train had a driver. Katei explained to him that this was a safety and public relations feature. The shuttle coaches travel relatively slowly and even if there were to be an accident it would not be too severe. The express trains on the other hand travel very fast to a limited number of stations, and it is considered safer to have a human in charge. Of course there are also some people who still won't get on a driver-less train.

They got on the train and travelled down the line quickly past several stations before the train stopped. Morton was a bit confused by this as they had gone right past their stop. Katei assured him that there was no problem, as all they had to do was cross over to the other side where a shuttle was waiting, and they would be back in a few minutes. This in fact was the case and they were soon at Morton's home station.

They decided it was easiest to walk from the station to Morton's home. The bike that Morton had left at the station on his way in had long gone. "Weird!" said Morton. "What's that?" asked Katei. "Well," said Morton, "it only seems like a few days ago that I left it here, and I feel like I should report its loss."

Morton and Katei gently strolled through the town to Morton's house, with Morton deep in thought, and slightly disorientated by his now not quite so familiar surroundings.

VI

Home

The walk back to Morton's abode was uneventful. Katei was unsure of how they were going to gain entry to the house. Morton had already been mulling this over for a few minutes, along with other things.

The house door was keyed to Morton's passport, and 'spare' ID cards, but was also dependent on his retina pattern. He was worried that the time in the stasis machine may have disrupted his eyes. He finally verbalised his concerns to Katei, who now also mulled over the problem as they strolled up to Morton's dwelling.

Katei examined the scanning device at Morton's doorway. She was surprised at how primitive it was. She fished around in her pocket, and withdrew her mobile phone.

She cleared her throat, and said to Morton, "As it happens, for some reason I still have a high definition, semi-holographic facial photograph of you stored on a memory slice in my phone." She called up the image, and magnified the image of the eye to the same size as Morton's eye. She held this in front of the scanner.

Morton gave the door a command word, and the entry LED glowed green, indicating that the door was now open. Morton meanwhile failed to grasp the significance of a woman keeping hold of a fellow's photographic image for a number of years. This was slightly to Katei's relief, but more to her annoyance.

Morton now in the familiar surroundings of home began to relax slightly. He felt rather confused, and decided that perhaps he had better sit down and review the situation. Katei followed him through to the living area. Morton took a deep sigh and his favourite seat. He looked quizzically at Katei, realising how much older she now looked. Less delicate he thought, more rounded, but rounded in a pleasant way. She was definitely more pleasing to the eye than the very delicate elf she had appeared before (in his opinion anyway) Morton mused.

He tried to fathom why what had happened to him had happened, and started to open his mouth to speak to Katei. Katei pre-empted his vocalisation, with a probably more sensible one of her own. "Tea, coffee, or perhaps something stronger?" she enquired. Morton momentarily considered the stronger option, but found himself asking for a strong cup of tea, and "only a tiny dash of that vile milk substitute stuff," adding "please" as he realised that he may have been a bit stern in his tone, and wanted to regain a polite stance.

As his listened to the water in the micro-kettle starting to pop, the steam heating and washing out the tea, he mused on the processes that his body had gone through, and how it was that he had woken up in the lab several years later than planned. Could his friend really have been the instigator he wondered, or was there something deeper involved in it?

Katei placed the tea on the table in front of Morton, and gently sipped from her own cup of black coffee. She made a mental note that someone needed to invent a milk substitute that tasted any good. She also worried that although the powdered milk was in a sealed container, that it was, after all, probably several years old.

The tea kick-started Morton's brain into further action, and had a similar effect on his insides. He managed to suppress a burp at the mouth end, but was unable to suppress some wind from another aperture. He felt himself redden slightly – he felt that Katei might not be finding him the gentleman he tried to be. He coughed loudly, and started to speak again, the words coming out in batches. "Now yesterday," he started, "No, err last umm... ah, some time ago." He brain was struggling to find a word to describe the state of waking after a Rip Van Winkle type sleep, indeed one of the directions his mind went in was the story of the aforesaid man. Katei realising his predicament suggested that as they were both in the business of inventing that they should invent a new word to describe the condition.

"Anabiosis," said Morton, "that's a good word," Katei laughed, and asked him to explain. "It does sound very good, but where did you get it from?" "It's a real word," Morton replied, "it just seemed to be very apt in this case."

"So," trailed Katei, "what of your partner then? Mr Barton." Morton creased his brow, as he thought. The thoughts somehow caused him to squint with the effort of thinking. Katei caught this expression on Morton's face, and imagined that he was somehow trying to see with his eyes, what had happened.

Meanwhile Katei sidled over to the keyboard of the computer in the room. She tried to think of some excuse to look up the word, that Morton had just 'invented'. In the end she gave up, and broke through his reverie to ask him if he would mind her looking the word up. He replied with a laugh, asking her to go ahead.

* A restoring to life from a deathlike condition; resuscitation.
* A state of suspended animation, especially one in which certain aquatic invertebrates are able to survive long periods of drought.
* From Greek anabiōsis return to life, from anabioun to return to life, from ana- + bioun to live, from bios life.

"Ah," breathed Katei, "so you feel that you have been dead, not just sleeping?" "Well," Morton replied, "given that the electric to the basement was to be turned off, I think someone might have preferred it if I was dead. But I cannot imagine that Paul would do such a thing to me." He paused, looking at Katei quizzically, "Would he?"

Katei having never been very fond of Paul Barton was at a slight loss for words. She wondered if her dislike was purely prejudice on her part, some kind of intuition, or what? She tried to explain this to Morton, but ended up not explaining it at all well. She started to explain how he reminded her of a rather slimy frog, or toad-like being hopping about. She got confused as she explained this, as she recalled an image of Morton in the stasis machine, looking very green. "So,", Morton said, "you think he is just a rather bad tadpole egg then?"

"Well!" he exclaimed, suddenly becoming more animated. "Lets see what we can find out about Paul." He pulled up a chair next to the computer that Katei was now sitting at. "Let's see if he is devil's spawn, or otherwise angel's eggs?" he muttered.

VII

Homework

Katei got up and had a look around the room, as Morton set to work running his fingers across the keyboard, and causing a racket of key clacking. Morton also issued forth various imprecations about versions of software, and access problems. Katei could sense that he was becoming very frustrated. "I am afraid your computer is now somewhat out of date with what is currently available on public networks," she sympathised. "I only bought this phone-cum-Travinetter a couple of months ago, and already it's out of date," she said, trying to alleviate his frustration somewhat.

Morton pondered for a bit. "Anyway," he said, "what are we going to eat?" Katei suggested that perhaps Morton might like to call up a home shopping web site. Morton took this advice, only to find that his ID and passwords were rejected. He had to return to the front of the house to look through the paper that was flowing from the letterbox. Eventually he found a recent issue of a credit card, and set about signing up for home shopping, only to find that he needed a shopper's dongle to access the local store. Katei tried to hide her amusement at Morton's frustration with the technology that he normally promoted, and proposed that she take a low tech walk to the nearest auto service station for some essentials. Morton agreed that that might be easier.

While she was away Morton pondered on how to track down Paul, and find out what had happened. It occurred to him that just as Katei had had to go out to find food, that he might have to do some travelling to find his quarry. While he mused on this, he walked around the house checking to see what was still working, ending up upstairs in the bathroom, checking that the hot water supply was still operational.

As he watched the system rinsing the bath, he became aware that someone was watching over his shoulder. That someone was Katei, having returned from gathering the required essentials. Katei looked at the bath fascinated. The bath looked a bit Jacuzzi-like, but also had several showerheads that moved. Morton explained that he had been experimenting with high-level bubble baths, where the user could soak in a sea of bubbles that could envelop a person's face, and still allow them to breath. This was achieved through a combination of air tanks, and a special thin film detergent. Morton went on to expand on how he had worked on the details with Paul Barton. The project has started as a medical one. The object had been to allow a person's lungs to be coated with what can only be described as cleaning fluid. The idea had then progressed into more prosaic uses.

Katei listened with interest to Morton's recounting of how they had developed the system. After he had finished with some musings on parts of the design, she asked him how it had been, working alongside his erstwhile friend. Morton replied that it had been occupying his mind, as to why Paul should have taken against him. He regarded it as very odd, seeing as how the pair of them had had such an intimate grasp of each other's minds. For her part Katei was feeling a growing jealousy towards the fellow she had never liked; Paul Barton. "He wasn't gay was he?" she asked, almost involuntarily (she was fighting some strange feelings, and immediately regretted the question. Morton, his mind still elsewhere, muttered, "No... No... I don't know. Never occurred to me to think about it."

Morton followed Katei down the passageway back to the room that contained Morton's equipment. Morton sat in an easy chair, while Katei continued on into the kitchen area. Morton had offered to prepare something to eat, but Katei protested that she had done the shopping, and knew what was there to use. Katei brought a large gin and tonic in for Morton. "The gin looked fine," she said, "but the tonics were way past sell-by-date." Having seen both in the fridge before going out, she had guessed that it would be a good idea to buy some more tonics.

As he sipped his drink Morton examined Katei's Travinetter. "Ah!" he exclaimed, "you have a U.S.B. four interface here!" Morton rummaged around in a drawer, and found a blue and orange coloured lead. He plugged one end into his Personal Computer, and the other into the Travinetter. "A bit like converting my PC to a Dumb Terminal," he said, "but it should do the trick!" This time he tapped more contentedly away at the keyboard, and was there making happy sounds, when Katei returned from preparing something to eat.

Morton continued to tap away at the keyboard with one finger as he consumed his plate of couscous and lamb, and sipped at a glass of Rioja. Katei moved a chair over next to Morton, so that she could see what he was doing. Morton had on one side of the screen details from an electoral roll that he had extracted from a web site containing credit details on people, and on the other side of the screen he was busy obtaining access to another company. Katei asked him what he was doing. Morton explained that the government had some time ago asked that all communications companies should have a monitoring point that agencies nominated by the government should have access to. "What I am attempting to do," he said, pausing slightly between words as he concentrated on what he was doing, "is to find one of those agencies that has access to the secure tap, and does not have proper security on its external access." "But how did you get someone else's details?" Katei asked. "I just got your device to lie about who owned it," replied Morton.

Katei watched as Morton worked through a number of internet addresses. Suddenly he exclaimed "Ah!" and then "Bingo Bongo!" as he turned to Katei and said, "I have it, this government agency worked with the Foundation a while back, and had to be warned about using the same passwords everywhere." A few keystrokes later Morton moved back from the screen. He turned around with his meal, and his drink, and proceeded to finish both. "Right," he whispered to Katei, "let's see if we can locate his mobile phone, Paul would never be without one." Morton went on to explain that once he had found the phone operator that Barton used, he would be able to bring up the tropism records. These records would show where a mobile phone had passed through in the last year.

It did not take Morton long to find the records he needed. He had refined the records that he had obtained from the system to provide him with a map of Barton's usual movements. From the map he could see that Barton appeared to stay overnight at one location, and travel to another location on most weekdays. There were gaps in some of the travel records though that Morton did not understand. He showed Katei the results of his work.

"So," said Katei, "you know where he is most of the time." She paused for a moment, and then said, "So what are you going to do about it?" "Well..." drawled Morton, "I think I might just follow him for a day, and see what he gets up to. But before that I will need to upgrade my equipment here, as using it the way that I am makes some of my research long winded." Morton went on to explain that he had tried to follow what Barton was up to in real time, but his equipment was just not fast enough to cope with the amount of data, and the number of calculations necessary to build a proper picture.

Katei asked Morton what is was he wanted to do. Morton started to walk around the room, his brow wrinkling, echoing the wrinkling of the thoughts in his mind. "I want to know what Paul is up to, and whom he is meeting," he said. He went on, "but it's much easier to do that electronically than by following him." Morton walked around the room a bit more, and then said, "It's interesting that he has a form of enhanced Bluetooth on his mobile phone. I've been able to get phone numbers and other information from his phone, and have also been able to scan the phones of people around him. What is also interesting is that the phone is picking up the RF-ID tags that are in the clothing of people around him.

"RFID?" queried Katei, raising her eyebrows. "Yes," Morton said, "the tags that are sewn into clothing, and pressed into other items by manufacturers." "Ah yes!" exclaimed Katei, "the thing that has replaced bar codes on supermarket products, but I had never thought that snooping on what Tig-Tags people had on them would become so popular. You don't just have to have the designer label now; you have to have the appropriate Tig-Tag."

"Anyway," sighed Morton, "I am quite tired now, and I think I need to turn in for a good night's sleep." "Me too" yawned Katei. "I use the bedroom at the back of the house" said Morton, "you should find all you need in one of the front bedrooms. I am afraid that you will have to use the main bathroom as only the back room has its own."

The two made their weary way to bed.

VIII

Home Discomforts

Morton was up early in the morning, and as soon has he had performed his morning ablutions, he made sure that Katei was having breakfast then went out to the garage to make sure that the fuel cell in his car was still active. He wished that he had done this the night before, although he was not sure what he would have done differently, if the cell was now incapable of holding a charge. As it was, the vehicle was in excellent condition, and the electronic registration details were all up-to-date.

"Now then," Katei asked Morton, "are you sure that you do not need me to help?" "I am sure I can cope," said Morton, in a positive voice, even though he had some nagging misgivings about what a few years' inflation might have done to prices. "If I think I am being ripped-off, I will call you and check," he said as he got into the car. Katei watched him drive off down the road, and then went back into the house.

Katei had eaten breakfast while wrapped in a dressing gown, and having cleared away the breakfast accoutrements she went upstairs to the bathroom. Here she decided that she would try out the enveloping bubble

44

bath. The bathroom was also equipped with a music system from which she selected some soothing songs to play. Katei luxuriated in the bath, marvelling at the way the foam enveloped her, but she could still breath. After about an hour of appreciating the warmth and the bathroom sound system, Katei thought she had better get out.

As Katei emerged from the bubbles she could hear the sound of voices outside of the window. "Aye," a voice said, "this is the place, to be sure. The geezer has gone off, but we may be able to force some information out of the bird he left behind." Katei was awfully certain that she did not fancy having information forced from her. She wondered how she might escape from the house. She got out of the bath and went into Morton's room at the back of the house. There was a large window in the room, leading to a balcony at the back. Katei gently pushed the window open, and looked out onto the balcony.

Katei breathed a sigh of relief as she spotted a spiral staircase leading down from the balcony. She quickly returned to the bathroom and extracted her clothes from the washer dryer where she had placed them earlier. She then crept back to the balcony. As she eased the window open she saw a burly man enter the back garden. She turned around to see where she could hide in the house, and started slightly as she saw the mess that the water mixture had made of the carpet; she had left big watery footprints up to the window, and then a large watery smudge by the window.

As Katei pondered the footprints she could hear someone breaking glass downstairs. She knew that the reinforced glass would take a while to get through, but also was very aware that within five or ten minutes some potential interrogators would be entering the house. Having seen the burly man out the back of the house, she was even more sure that having information forced from here was not a nice idea.

IX

Intrusion Detection

It did not take Morton long to reach the outskirts of town where the computer shop was located. He had been a bit flummoxed by a new road layout, and uncertain why parts of the road had a different coloured surface. He had been pleased to find that the parking bays for smaller cars were located close to the store that he wanted to visit.

He took his time browsing through items in the store, carefully reading through descriptions on the boxes. The store had an Internet Café style bar at the back, to which Morton retired after spending a bit less than an hour looking at items. He got himself a soft drink, and booked a terminal. He used this to update himself with the use of the latest equipment. Once he had completed his research, he was able to return to the main body of the store, with a good grasp of what he needed. He mused to himself that is was just as well electronic equipment was forever getting smaller, or he might not have been able to fit it all in his car.

One of the sales assistants gave Morton a hand to take his purchases out to the car. The assistant took some interest in the car. "Very early model this!" he exclaimed, "You must have been one of the first people to buy a car powered by a iron fuel cell." The assistant turned out to be a bit of a geek as far as cars were concerned, and wanted to look at various bits of the car. Normally Morton would be only too pleased to talk technology, but he wanted to get back home, and was also a little worried that he needed some more education in the latest cars, an education that he did not want from the assistant who was becoming more of a geek by the minute.

He finally managed to stop the assistant talking by telling him that he had an important private call to make, and he needed to use the system in the car, as his mobile phone's Bluetooth communications was playing up. Of course the geek wanted to fix this for Morton, but he finally managed to get in the car. As he sat there the geek turned around to watch him. Morton decided that he would go through the motions of making a phone call, and he thought what better than to phone home, and tell Katei to pop some glasses in the freezer, so that he could have a good cold gin and tonic when he got back.

The ringing tone seemed to go on for long time. Morton wondered if Katei has gone out, or was in the garden out of reach of the phone. Finally the computer picked the call up, and started to speak in Morton's voice. Morton pressed the combination of phone keys to switch the computer into video, and speakerphone mode. The display paper in his car having been unused for some time took a while to generate an image. If the geek had still been looking he would have seen Morton's brow crinkled in puzzlement.

The web-cam attached to the computer was pointed at the back window of his house. The window had become opaque, and seemed to be undulating. As he watched a small black hole appeared in the window. The hole lengthened into what looked like a slit, until Morton realised that what he was looking at was someone using a pair off tin-snips to cut their way into his house. The snips were cutting through the laminate of the shattered window.

Morton could not think of what to do. This sort of thing was right outside of his normal experience of the world. He watched aghast, as the window suddenly ripped open, and several large men came tumbling in. He could hear them speaking, cursing at the suddenness of their entry through the weakened window that they had been leaning on. He heard one of the men say, "This must be the equipment that he is using to sneak on us. Let's smash all of this bleeding stuff up. We can smash the fucking geezer up later."

Because the image was so indistinct, he could not make out who was talking, though he thought it was a man who had a rather big head. He heard another man, who he guessed was the one with the beard say in a squeaky voice, "Yeah mate, I bet 'e did'in know that we was sneaking back on 't ares'ole." Morton shuddered, and wondered where Katei might be. He guessed that what the thug was saying was that he had been caught monitoring their communications. Morton suddenly realised that he should have phoned the police immediately. He put the call to his house on hold, and dialled 999. A recorded voice thanked him for his call, and informed that the service had been discontinued in the interests of the public." Morton let the rest of the message get as far as telling him that he should re-dial using 112 for general emergencies. He dialled 112, and was then required to key the number of the appropriate service, or hold for an operator. It did not take long for an operator to come on the line, but it did take a long time for Morton to explain what was going on.

Eventually the emergency operator agreed with him that the police should be despatched to his home to find out what was going on. Having got this far Morton was then put through to a police operator, who could not believe that Morton could not remember his postcode, and that they would have to find his house, by his address. The police warned Morton not to approach his house, until they told him it was safe to do so, and then proceeded to ask Morton questions about his ethnicity so that a complete report could be filed.

Morton switched the call back to the house where a lot of noise was being made. One of the men was shouting "Oy! Hurry up and find that bird we ain't got all day, and I is looking forward to a bit o' interrogation like." Morton decided that despite what the police had told him, he was going to go to his house, and see what he could do. He left the speaker going as he drove, and could hear equipment being broken, and the men calling to each other about where the 'bird' had flown to. The consensus of opinion among the men seemed to be that she had escaped out the back, and the last thing he heard from his computer before it too must have been smashed, was the men kicking their way back out of the window.

As he approached the house he could hear police sirens wailing. As he rounded a bend a large North American MPV came careering around the corner. One of the men in the front had a head that looked too large for his body, and the other a beard. Morton realised that this must be the gang of men escaping. They too had probably heard the police siren, and had made good their escape. Morton fervently hoped that they had escaped without having found their 'bird' Katei.

As Morton approached his house, he could see a police vehicle parked outside. An officer was there speaking into his lapel, and Morton could see another, taller, officer pressing the doorbell. The policeman who was speaking into his shirt caught sight of Morton. "Sorry sir," he said, "we are investigating a potential incident, would you mind moving on?" After spluttering slightly Morton managed to explain that it was his house. "In that case Sir," the policeman said, "it would be useful to us if you could produce some identification." Morton was not quite sure what to do at this juncture; as of course he was using one of his 'special' ID's.

While Morton stood there with a dumb look on his face, composing an explanation in his head to give to the policemen, an upstairs window had opened. Katei covered in a bathrobe was waving at the party below. "Morton!" she shouted, "I am so glad you are here." "Excuse me Madam," the taller policeman said, "we are investigating a reported incident, and I will have to ask you some questions." "Never mind the sodding questions!" shouted Katei, "just get around the back, and check that there are no more thugs out there." "All in good time," growled the police officer, "we must make sure that we follow the proper procedure for your safety."

X

Post Procedure

Once the police had completed their procedures Morton and Katei were able to set about tidying up the mess that the thugs had made. The police had provided Morton with the phone number of an emergency glazier, who had arrived and boarded up the damaged area.

Morton opined that before they tackled the debris-strewn room they should sit down and have a strong cup of coffee. Once Morton had made the coffee, he joined Katei at the breakfast bar in the kitchen. "Well," said Morton, "that was a lucky escape, just as well the police got here." "Some luck!" exclaimed Katei, "they were gone before the police arrived." Katei went on to explain that she had retraced her footsteps backwards to the bathroom, and had re-entered the bubbles. The intruders had seen the footsteps leading to the fire escape, and had assumed that she had run out into the garden somewhere. It had not occurred to them that someone might be ensconced in the bubbles.

After having chatted about the incident for a bit longer, and thrown out broken equipment, the two agreed that it might be safer if they were to make their way to Katei's place. "Much of the equipment that they have destroyed was pretty useless anyway," said Morton. Katei asked Morton what they should do with the equipment that he had just bought. Between them they decided that the heavier things could be brought in to replace the outdated and damaged parts. The lighter but useful bits they would take to Katei's house.

The new equipment was set up fairly quickly, and by the time it was ready for Morton to load some new software onto it, a local tradesman had arrived to board up and secure the glass destroyed by the intruders. Morton was still quite dusty from cleaning up the mess that had been left. He was so intent on the loading of new programs that he did not notice the dust or the tradesman. The man remarked to Katei, "That scruffy gent is a bit of a rude old bugger. Don't say hello or nothing." Katei explained it away by telling the man that Morton was a bit trau-matised. The man gave Katei two cards explaining that both his cousins were very learned, had been to univer-sity, and now both ran counselling services. "Very cheap." The man left still looking over his shoulder at the preoccupied Morton. Katei let out a sigh. She thought that if anybody was traumatised, it was herself.

As Morton was plugging in the final components Katei asked him how it might be that the intruders had picked on the house to attack. "I think it was my fault," said Morton "I was probably a bit slap dock in the way that I was checking up on Paul." "How's that?" asked Katei. "Well," said Morton, "I could have been a bit more circumspect with my probes. Anyone who was concerned about being snooped upon, would have been monitoring the access taps to the system, and realised that someone was accessing their data." Katei puckered her brow, and looked at Morton, "But," she said, "I thought you were using Government tap points." Morton raised an eyebrow and said, "Yes, Government tap points, but the software reports those access attempts to local log files – these people were able to watch us watching them. Which makes me think that Paul Barton must have had a hand in this."

Morton fiddled around with the software, making sure that the components of the software matched the new and old hardware that he had purchased. After much mild cursing, he uttered a cry of delight. The sound made Katei start. "What's wrong?" she exclaimed. "Not wrong," said Morton, "it's dead right!" Katei walked over and looked over Morton's shoulder. He was looking at a combination of text and pictures. "Ah," said Katei, "I see, you have entered the system at a lower level." "Yes," said Morton "Luckily I backed up the data I collected earlier onto my memory stick pen storage. It had the phone company's analogue access lines details and logon details. I have logged into one of the Base Station Controllers near where he appeared to be, and have been waiting for Paul's phone to become active so that I could get a more definite location by triangulation with other Base Stations."

Katei went to point at an item on the screen, but had her finger batted away by Morton. "Ouch!" whimpered Katei. "Sorry," said Morton, "lovely new screen, and it would be a shame to get finger grease on it." He passed the mouse over to Katei, and suggested that she use it to move the cursor arrow to point at things on the screen. Katei used the mouse to point at some items and went on to query Morton. "I understand the way you have located the BSC and the Base stations, and the point that Barton is at. But what is the rather hazy picture further down?" Morton took the mouse back, and clicked it several time to re-visit some of the items he had set up earlier. He explained to Katei. "Having got access to the base station, I have been varying the signal to Paul's phone. In fact, as he has a 'quad band' phone I have been able to do a bit more than that, and have been able to modulate the four different signals. I have also been able to collect the weaker signals echoing back from Paul and the room that he is in. It is a technique that I tried to use some time back for medical people to look inside the heads of people using mobile phones. The technology has advanced so much, I can almost map out the room that he is in."

Katei took the mouse back, and clicked through the images that Morton had saved. With Morton's approval, she dropped some of the images into some 3D imaging software. They could see the room that Barton was in, and they could also see indistinct lumps that were presumably other people in the room. Having mused over the images for a while Katei returned to the last image which was the clearest, and showed the inside of Barton's head. "That man needs a doctor!" expostulated Katei. Morton looked at her quizzically. "Well I reckon he has gone off his rickety rocker if you ask me," said Morton. "No, No..." Katei said, as she searched for words. "What I mean is that the inside of his head is wrong," explained Katei. "I did a lot of research into this type of thing when I was creating the non-gravity effect. What is inside his head looks wrong."

Katei sent some images to the printer, and Morton took over the mouse again. When Katei arrived back from the printer, Morton was just removing his memory stick from a socket in the computer. Katei looked at the screen, where various items of clothing were displayed. "Going shopping?" she asked. "No," laughed Morton, "this is what the people in the room were wearing." Katei laughed too. "How did you cotton on to that!" she said. "Picking up people's Tig-Tags is all the rage at the moment." "Well," said Morton, "I could see that the capacity is there, but I have no real idea of why anyone should want it."

Katei explained that it all started with manufactures realising that people showing designer labels on the outside was to some extent naff, especially on expensive items, and that a more subtle approach could be obtained by the use of Radio Frequency Identifier tags; RFID's or Tig-Tags as they had become known. In a similar way that the mobile phone Bluetooth system can be used to see who has a phone in a room, phones had options added to detect what RFID tags were in range. "For example," she said, "the shirt you are wearing is made by M and S, your shoes are Cartier, but either you are wearing no socks and undies, or they are too old to have RFID tags in them." Morton peered at Katei's phone. The details were shown on the display. Morton took the phone, and scrolled down the list displayed. He blushed, and handed the phone back. Katei looked at him and raised her eyebrows. "Well," said Morton, "all designer stuff you have, including what looks to be some quite expensive and," he coughed, "interesting underwear." "You see!" cried Katei, "a good game eh?"

XI

Return to Suspenders

Morton and Katei set off for the City early in the morning. A grey dawn had turned into a grey drizzle. They
boarded a slow train to the next express station. The
express did not take long to arrive, and they were soon
on their way to Katei's London apartment.

Morton gently extracted his new 'Ready News' display
paper from its holder, and unfolded it. The device had
already picked up the day's news, and Morton started to
read through it. Katei gently dozed, the slight rocking of
the train having lulled her back into wanting to sleep. She
was rudely awoken by an exclamation from Morton. He
had reached the financial section of the 'Ready News',
and there was speculation about the sale of the Pescod
Foundation. The analysts were trying to work out how
this had come about for such a stable organisation. The
way that the deal looked was that many staff would be
lost, and the main assets sold. The people that stood to
loose the most were the people that worked there, and
had a large part of their salary paid by share dividends.
There was also speculation as to why Morton Elise had
totally ceased dealing in shares suddenly. It was well
known that he had slowed up in trading a year before,

and speculation was rife. There was also speculation about Paul Barton who was assumed to have a lot of money, but none of it appeared traceable.

Morton muttered away for several minutes about how he should have set up his dealing system again. Katei tried to talk him out of blaming himself for not reinstating the system. At one point Morton was all for going back to reconstruct his system. Katei managed to persuade him that it would not be safe to return to his house for two reasons. First there was the worrying thought that the thugs might return, and second that the Police would be back to make further enquires, and it might turn out a bit awkward, as Morton was no longer in possession of a valid ID card. Morton finally acquiesced, by which time they had reached the London main line station.

Morton stood in front of a map of the Underground for a long time, his brow at times wrinkled in concentration. Katei's brow was also wrinkled, but in frustration at Morton's tardiness. Suddenly he turned round to Katei. "Is your phone turned on", he almost snapped at her. Katei jumped and stuttered "Well... yes." "Turn it off," he said, "people may have already traced you to here, I am a damn fool for forgetting your phone." Morton explained that the new unit that he had procured, he had purchased with cash so that the phone would not be easily traceable to him. Meanwhile Katei's phone had been transmitting their journey. Katei was just about to turn her phone off, when Morton suddenly changed his mind. "No," he said, "perhaps it will be a useful decoy. Let's leave your phone on, and post it back to my house. That ought to confuse anyone attempting to spy on us."

It was a fairly simple task to obtain wrapping paper at the station, and to use the post office located there. They also bought another phone for Katei at a convenient shop, using cash to pay for it. Morton also bought an Underground map with both a schematic diagram, and a geographical layout of stations. Their transactions completed, they then headed for the Underground, and made their way to Katei's flat. During the journey Morton kept irritating Katei, by completely unfolding the map, and poking at it with a marker pen. Katei was quite relieved to arrive at the station near her apartment.

On arrival at her flat, she and Morton were really glad to be able to dump their rucksacks on the table. Light though the equipment was, it had been an exacting chore to manoeuvre through the throng of people on the Underground. They both decided that tea and biscuits were in order, and Katei set about organizing this while Morton unpacked the rucksacks and made little "tut tut" noises about some of the equipment. When Katei had got the tea and biscuits ready she made Morton sit down and relax. As they sipped their beverages, and nibbled on the biscuits, Katei had to explain to Morton how some of the bits of equipment interfaced together. This was due to Morton having missed out on a few years of advances in the technology.

Morton got up, and walked around the room. "I am not sure that we need all this stuff," he said, "with the computing power that you have in your computer here, and the stuff that I have got stored from my previous investigations, I think that we may have sufficient information anyway." Morton took the map out again, and started to flap it about, much to Katei's displeasure. "We need a plan," he said. "A plan to get Paul alone, and find out just what is going on." Katei managed to persuade Morton that he did not have to rush off at that moment and do something, but should perhaps rest for a while and clear his mind. "Perhaps play a game or something?"

"Scrabble!" he said, and lunged toward the computer. "Stop!" exclaimed Katei, "No!" Morton pulled up short and turned round. Katei had gone red at the way she had shouted at him. She could see that Morton was upset and confused. Upset that his erstwhile best friend had tried to wipe him out, and confused by being in stasis for several years. Katei went over to a cupboard, and fetched out a board version of Scrabble. "Old fashioned I know!" she said, "but I think you need a break from a computer screen, and perhaps having to actually pick up the tiles and put them down will relax you a bit." Katei arranged the board on a table between two easy chairs, and then fetched a bottle of wine. "Maybe this will help relax you too," she said.

The game took them up to lunchtime. By this time the break, and perhaps the wine, as they had to open a second bottle, had relaxed Morton. During the game his brain had still been working, and he announced that he now had at least half a plan, but that they might as well go and find a reasonable place for lunch first before he did a small bit of shopping.

Both Morton and Katei were worried about unwelcome visitors, and before they left for lunch Morton took a look around the apartment for some ideas as to either detect or deter intruders. He spent a while examining Katei's gravity experiment. Katei showed him some of the improvements she had made. She explained that the fundamental graviton particle types, "W and Z Bosons are just fine, with evidence of gluons." Morton asked what the function of the photon transmitter was. Katei explained that she had found a peculiar interaction between gravity and electromagnetism, and had been following up some data gained from sunspot activity where gravity could be seen to be containing magnetic forces. Her further work meant that the gravity 'Suspense Suit' could be done away with, as the effect was now far more powerful.

"I have an idea," said Morton. "How about if we relocate what you call your suspenders next to the entrance?" "An interesting idea!" replied Katei, "but with an absence of gravity there, how are we going to get in and out? And if we can get in and out so can others." Morton was sitting at the console, and brought up the screen that had the electromagnetic setting on it. "Big electromagnet?" he asked. Katei looked puzzled for a moment, and then said "Ah! I see what you mean. Make the area gravity free, but use the photon and graviton interaction to keep people held there. But still the question remains, how to we get in and out?" "Rope," said Morton.

Katei took a while to find some rope. She and Morton then affixed either end at the extremities of the suspense field that they had created. They had to experiment for a bit to get the balance right, so that someone unsuspecting entering the apartment would be captured and gently be taken to the middle of the field. Morton experimented with throwing heavy items forward to see if that would give enough of a force to move him out of the field. In the end they got it just right, so that if one did not pick up the rope from the floor, and use it to get across the field, one was effectively trapped.

XII

Shopping

Morton let Katei choose where to go for lunch, as he did not know the area too well, and quite a few things had changed anyway. Katei picked a place that served only vegetarian food. Morton was not quite convinced at first, but in the end quite enjoyed his meal. "Anyway," said Katei, "what with the price of meat nowadays I think a lot of people are eating less of it." Morton tried to reply, but he still had a bit of sun-dried tomato bread in his mouth, and could only make "Humph" noises. Once he had eaten and swallowed, he said, "Yes, I have always liked to have less, better quality meat, rather than mass-produced muck. But whatever this juice is it seems to make you go to the loo a lot." Katei raised her eyebrows and said, "Nothing to do with nearly a bottle and a half of Vinho Verde then?" Morton was not sure whether the question needed a reply or not, and in the event kept quiet.

"What do we need to buy then?" Katei asked Morton. "Well for a start, I would like to get hold of a dual purpose multi-layer printer," said Morton. "Dual purpose?" asked Katei. "Yes," said Morton, "I want to be able to copy a plastic key and an ordinary metal key.

The metal key will be copied in polymer of course, but it should still do at least one job. Once we have found where Paul is we need to be able to get into the building without being noticed." Morton then went on to explain that a special bit of the Underground passed near where he had located Paul, and it might come in handy to use it. Katei was not too sure what Morton was talking about. She decided that in the course of time it would all become clear.

They left the little café, in a fairly pleasant mood. The weather being reasonably clement, they decided to take a gentle stroll to the area where they proposed shopping.

They took some time to find a shop that sold the type of printer that Morton wanted. The printer was of the type that prints in three dimensions. Instead of the printer producing ink from its print heads, it fired out a fast setting polymer. The printer could produce small items fairly quickly, and larger items over a period of time.

Having selected the appropriate printer, Morton went to the sales desk, and then waited while the assistant exited out the back to fetch the device. When she returned, Morton proffered his cash card in payment. The assistant took the card, and popped it in the card reader. "Oh!" she exclaimed, "that's a funny one." Morton raised an eyebrow. The assistant said, "I am sorry sir, but you need to also show some other ID to buy this, some sort of security thing." Morton reached into his pocket for the ID card, and then realised that he had the ID of Mr Tracy on him, not his real ID, and it would not match his credit card if he had to pay using that for further 'security'. "Ah," said Morton, "I am afraid that I do not have it with me, I will come back later and sort it out then." "All right Sir," said the assistant, "I'll put it back out the back for you to get later."

Morton left the shop with a bit of a frown on his face. "Stupid of me," he said, "I should have realised that such equipment would become regulated." Katei asked him why he did not use his credit card to make the purchase. Morton replied that he was worried about the transaction being traced back to him, and his whereabouts, by anyone with access to financial transaction records. "Actually," he said, "I am not even sure how anonymous cash top-up cards are either."

The post lunchtime sun was becoming quite hot on Morton's face, as they made their way toward the underground station that he had mentioned. This was useful as Morton was anxious, that they should be wearing dark glasses, and hats with sun visors so as to be not easily be recognised by CCTV. The equipment also gave them welcome relief from the hot sun.

"There we are," Morton said, and nodded to the front of him, "next to the newsagent." The frontage of the building looked a little different. The ground floor had obviously once been an underground station. The rest of the facades of the buildings around it made the red brickwork look out of place. The pair stopped in the newsagent when they reached it, and bought a newspaper and two ice-lollies.

On leaving the newsagent, Morton shuffled around to stand by a rather incongruous looking door. The area around it had been filled in, but was in need of a good lick of paint. Next to it were the jet black doors of, perhaps, a prestigious office. Morton looked all around the door, and then inserted a device that he had obtained from his earlier shopping expedition. Having done this Morton and Katei walked back in front of the newsagents, and began to retrace their steps to Katei's apartment.

XIII

A bit more Shopping

Morton and Katei had some fun and games getting back into Katei's apartment. Morton absent-mindedly forgot about the anti-gravity arrangement, and got caught in stasis part way into the room. Katei was able to rescue him using the rope. The ease with which Katei was able to rescue Morton caused them to rethink the way the trap was laid. They readjusted the field so that a third party could not pass the rope into the field. Katei managed to baffle Morton with talk of negative spin and super weight atoms induced into a carbon fibre rope. Between them they devised a special rescue rope made out of activated carbon fibre with a heavy noose on the end. This was placed out of sight above the porchway outside of Katei's apartment.

While Katei was making the changes to the security system, Morton had sat himself back at the computer, and was looking for locksmiths who had been prosecuted for illegally copying keys. He decided that a bit of good old-fashioned metalworking might be a bit easier to come across, than the effort that he might have to go to avoid being detected buying an up-to-date device. It took Morton about an hour to identify three likely people, and he then set off out on his own to find them. Morton was armed with a diagram of the inside of the lock produced by the device that he had earlier used to scan the lock.

The first individual that Morton tried got very suspicious of him. The man who had fiery red hair, long beard, and glasses that seemed too large, occupied a shop located inside a railway arch next to a main line station. The fellow took a look at the drawings that Morton had printed out and said, "Ere mate, what are you? A beeding Pain Close Cop or sommat?" He refused to talk to Morton any further, apart from to say "Bastard!" and "Peedle Off!" a lot. Morton decided to leave swiftly before the man got too annoyed. He suspected that the fellow would not have attacked a plain clothes policeman, but he was not going to take any chances.

The second establishment that Morton tried, was a bit more helpful. The shop was the only one left in a redevelopment area. The proprietor was very co-operative. He pointed out some of the security nuances of the lock, and showed Morton a template of the type of key that he would have to use. "Special key that mate," he said, "stuff what the big national security type use."

Morton asked how much it would cost to produce. The proprietor, who had short white hair, and a very pointy nose, replied "Nah! Sorry mate. A nice little earner, but not for me." He explained to Morton that the shop had been compulsory purchased for a tidy sum, and he was going straight, and not taking on any more "funny stuff." "I done enough time, and bleeding rehabilitations already," he said. He went on to say that he should have already retired, and was eagerly looking forward to it.

He sketched in some of the further detail required on Morton's printout with a pencil.

After he had left the second shop, Morton made some further notes on his printout, with the pencil that the owner of the shop had given him. Morton felt slightly annoyed with himself that his drawing and writing was so bad. Morton had hardly ever used a pen or pencil, even at school. He mused that it was quite different to using a drawing stylus on personal organiser display paper, where the computer corrected the mistakes for one, straightened lines, and produced rounded edges.

The third place that Morton tried was in the back of a department store. Here a tiny unit was run by a small, pleasantly spoken little man, who kept calling Morton "Sir". He kept repeating, "No job is too much trouble." The man agreed to produce the key there and then, but for a reasonably large sum of money. He told Morton that it was expensive due to the "liabilities that producing such a key could land one with Sir!"

While Morton waited for the key to be produced he wandered about the store looking at other items. He had the feeling as he walked about that the security cameras were all pointing at him, but every time he looked carefully they all seemed to be pointing away. He decided that he was just feeling jittery due to the situation he was in.

Morton collected the key from the small man at the back of the shop without incident. He tried to leave the shop in a nonchalant manner, but still felt that every camera was watching him. He waited until he was half a mile away from the store, before he removed the key from his pocket and a paper bag to examine it. The key had been very well fabricated, and had a complicated system to enable a magnet to pull internal levers back that would release the tumblers when the key was turned. Morton pondered what type of lubrication the lock had to make sure that it would work.

Morton suddenly stopped examining the key, and looked around him, and was pleased to see that no security cameras were pointing at him. He put the key back in his pocket, and headed back to Katei's apartment.

XIV

A bit of Snooping

Morton tarried for some time outside the building that housed Katei's apartment. He was trying to make up his mind as to what specifics he could use to confront his colleague. Morton could not comprehend how it could be that his friend Paul would consign him to death. As he mused on this, he tossed the keys that he had recently purchased from hand to hand.

Katei, who had been awaiting Morton's return, wondered why Morton was hanging around the front of the building. She first thought to open a window and call to him, and then decided that she would watch, and wait to see what he might do. Morton though deep in his reverie was still vaguely aware of his surroundings, people, and vehicle movements. In fact what gradually sank into his brain was people's movements in two different vehicles. Having felt slightly paranoid about being looked at by cameras earlier, he now felt that these people were watching him.

Katei was surprised to see Morton suddenly scurry into the building, so quick that she did not have time to deactivate the household defence system that they had constructed. When she arrived downstairs Morton was gently floating about near the ceiling. Katei turned off the device from inside, and even though he was fore-warned, Morton landed on the floor in an undignified lump, and was not best impressed by Katei's laughter.

Morton made his way to the main room, trying to recon-struct his dignity while Katei switched the devices back on again. Once he had pulled himself together he explained his hurried return to the apartment. Katei did not know whether to just humour Morton or take him seriously. The events at Morton's house had been quite traumatic after all, she thought to herself.

"But why were you standing around in the street doing a juggling act with keys, and drawing attention to yourself in the first place?" asked Katei. "Paul Barton," said Morton. "I cannot believe that he would have tried to kill me. Maybe he didn't, but I would like an answer." "Well,", said Katei, "you had better come and see this then." Morton followed her to the adjoining room where Morton's computer equipment had been set up.

Katei explained to Morton that she had been busy while he was out, and had copied and altered some of the computer scripts that Morton had set up. She showed him how she had logged into three mobile phone base stations, and was able to triangulate onto Paul Barton's phone. "Furthermore," she said, "I have been able to pick up signals from phones very close to Barton." Morton looked though the logs with interest. Six of the people could be traced firmly to the USA and two were possibly from the New Republic of Pacifica.

"And another interesting thing you should see," said Katei, gently moving Morton away from the keyboard.

"I have been able to capture raw radio data from their phones, and I have also been able to swamp the room with radio signals of various wavelengths, and collect the signals back." Morton looked up fascinated as Katei brought up rough images of people and objects in the room. "People are the hardest to see properly," explained Katei, "as radio waves go through too easily and it needs quite fine tuning to pick them up properly."

"And now, my next clever trick," said Katei. "I rescued the logs from your house, and two of the individuals match those horrible people that broke in through the window. And some of the Tig-Tags match as well."

Morton moved back to the keyboard. He gently moved the pointer around the screen, zooming in and out, and flipping back to look at previously captured pictures. He pulled a chair over, and stared at the rather fuzzy picture of Paul Barton. The picture suddenly broke up and an even fuzzier picture appeared. "What happened?" asked Morton. "I think all of the people with phones have left the room," said Katei. "It looks like they are leaving Barton to make a private call."

As Morton and Katei watched, the image of an ear appeared on the screen. "Interesting!" said Katei. "At this proximity you could look inside Barton's head and see what makes him tick!" "Really?" asked Morton enthusiastically. "Silly!" said, Katei, "All you would see is brain mush." "No." Morton said, "I mean that seriously, I would like to see if his brain is correct." As Morton was so worried about his friend Katei thought that she had better take this seriously, and moved over, and took the chair to adjust the fine tuning of the system.

Katei had earlier downloaded from the Internet what was known as a descriptor file. This file described roughly where things should be inside a person. They watched the screen, and slice by slice, bit-by-bit an image of Paul Barton's brain appeared on the screen. Just as the last bit was about to appear tapering away to the neck, the screen flashed inverted and then back again. "Damn," said Katei, "I think we have been rumbled. The system has cut us off. Either that or a real maintenance technician needs the lines."

"Anyway," said Katei, "lets see what we captured." Katei arose from the chair, and pushed it out of the way so that Morton could get a look at the screen as well. "What's that black bit?" asked Morton. "Odd," said Katei wrinkling her brow slightly. "Is it where the system cut out?" asked Morton "No," replied Katei pushing Morton out of the way and regaining the chair.

Katei pounded away at the keyboard for a while, selecting new definition files from the Internet, and comparing them with the data received. Finally she looked up at Morton and said, "It's very dense matter, it looks like he has a well advanced brain tumour. That is why the radio waves were passing through it differently."

"Maybe," Morton said, and went quiet. After Morton had been quiet for some time Katei looked at him quizzically. "Perhaps that is why Paul is behaving so strangely? What is the rest of the deal? Who are these people? What danger could we be in? The type of stuff that Paul has access to, and the money he has could endanger the whole country!"

"Maybe this lump in his brain is the answer," he mused, "I have heard of people doing strange things due to tumours." Katei nodded in agreement with Morton, saying that she had had a great aunt who had become unstable. The aunt had eventually been diagnosed as having a brain tumour.

Katei looked on as Morton walked around the room, mostly in circles, not quite knowing what to say or do. "Right," Morton suddenly said, "we can carry on with something like my original plan, but we need to kidnap Paul, and get him to the facility that I was thinking of in the West Country. We are probably in danger here ourselves, and we must get Paul away, and find out what he has been up to with what are obviously evil men." "But how?" asked Katei, steadying her head as Morton finally stood still.

XV

But How

Morton had a very bad night's sleep. He finally managed to sleep for a couple of hours, but awoke not feeling in the slightest refreshed. A hot shower made him feel a bit better, but he was still pondering on his problem of how to collect Paul Barton. As he dressed he wondered what Katei had been able to achieve with the radio signals.

Morton found Katei in the kitchen making a pot of tea. "I heard you moving," she said, "so I thought that I should get the tea on." Katei could see from Morton's face that he had not slept well. "Perhaps you will need a whole pot full?" she asked half teasingly, and then regretting it because Morton looked so sad. "Perhaps some tea will stir my brain cells into action," said Morton, leaning against the work surface.

Morton took his cup of tea into the room with a computer. He tapped away; sipping his tea not realising that Katei kept topping it up from the teapot. When the teapot was empty and after Katei had poured the last drop into Morton's cup, Katei said to him, "Last stir of brain cells." Leaning over to look at the screen, she could see that Morton was looking at an article on steroids.

"You have an idea?" she asked. "Sort of," replied Morton. "I have looked at what we know about this tumour, and how it could be treated." He went on to explain that perhaps if they could administer the right type of steroids the tumour could be shrunk.

Morton and Katei spent the rest of the morning researching the tumour and the possible types of steroid. They also puzzled over how they could get it into Paul Barton. If indeed the tumour was causing Paul Barton to behave strangely, the steroids in alleviating that would aid their attempted 'rescue' of him. The only other thing that Katei came up with was drilling a hole in Barton's head to perhaps take the pressure off the brain.

They spent some time discussing how to obtain the items they needed and where to get them. Morton found a foreign website where he was could obtain both the steroid and a trephine device to make a hole in the skull. Morton said that he would order the trephine, "Just in case, and it's on the website anyway."

"OK" said Morton, "now we have to be outrageous." "Err, yes?" said Katei, with a very quizzical look on her face. "Ideas!" exclaimed Morton. "As many silly ideas as we can think of." "Ah," breathed Katei, feeling slightly relieved, but also a bit miffed that she could have thought of something much more outrageous. "You mean a bit of brainstorming?" she asked. "Just that!" enthused Morton. "Let's brainstorm this brain problem."

After spending some time getting nowhere, and having ideas that would just not work or were just too outrageous, Katei went back to look up the recommendations for taking Dexamethasone drugs and the like, and of the newer one that they had selected. The recommendation for the newer drug was that it could be taken with just water. The older drugs could cause abdominal discomfort and therefore had to be taken with food. "Can we somehow dose his water?" asked Katei. Morton looked glum. "How?" he said.

"Well," said Katei, "all of our ideas seem to have gone as cold as this wet weather has got." Morton looked out of the window at the pouring rain, and remarked on the fact that it seemed to have been very wet ever since he had been revived. Katei brought out a leaflet that urged people to decrease their carbon footprint. "Of course the UK produces next to nothing now compared to the rest of the world," Katei said. "We get bullied and taxed for it and the rest of the world carries on regardless. The doomsayers reckon the weather is all down to global warming."

Morton went over to the window and looked out into the street. "Looks like sleet," he said, "be dangerous if it turns to ice later." Morton pondered the street some more, and then shouted, "ICE!" This made Katei jump, and the top of the teapot that she was just taking to the kitchen jumped off and clattered to the floor. "Paul always has a rum at midday, and insists on a particular type of ice from the Arctic," Morton said. He went on to explain that it was a little quirky thing that Paul liked to do "to remember his seafaring ancestors in the World Wars... If we can get the medication into a consignment of his ice then we can control the dose. He always waits for the ice to melt in the rum, and then drinks it. He uses it to time how long his lunch break is. Pours it at the start, and then when it is water that is the end of lunch break, and he drinks it."

"That's if he still keeps to that routine," said Katei. "Let's not go that way," said Morton. "This ritual is so ingrained in him I don't think anything would stop it." Morton took up his ritual of walking around the room while he tried to get his thoughts together. He knew the shop that supplied the ice and he started to hatch a plan in his head: He would buy a sack of the ice for 'himself', and then find out from the shopkeeper when Paul was due his next consignment.

He explained his plan to Katei: They would doctor the ice that he brought back from the shop. Having found out when Paul was due his next consignment he would then go back to the shop for another one for 'himself' and offer to deliver the one to Paul as it was on the way. The only dangers in the plan were if the shopkeeper let Paul Barton know that he had seen Morton, or he was caught at the point of delivery. He was counting on being able to wear a fairly full hat or a hood (with the weather so cold and wet) to avoid being caught by any facial recognition cameras the company might have.

Morton need not have worried about the need for something to cover his head. The next few days saw a continuation of the bad weather that had been dogging the country for the past weeks. The summer hosepipe bans had quickly vanished. It also turned out that he had no worries over the purchasing of the ice. The normal retailer of the ice was on an early holiday, and the retailer's harassed, and overburdened assistant was only too pleased to let Morton deliver it. The assistant had been given strict orders from his boss to see that it was personally delivered, and not sent by mail or courier.

The bored receptionist at the front desk of the offices where Paul Barton was ensconced took no real notice of a cyclist (Morton) delivering the ice. She snapped at him about 'trivial matters of ice' when Morton tried to explain what it was all about. She explained that she had so many important items to be getting on with. She did though immediately contact the relevant office for the consignment to be collected. She then returned to busying herself with the computer on her desk. Morton stepped back out of the way, and watched the lift lights indicate descent from the top floor, the collection of the ice, and the return of the lift to the top floor. As he stepped even further back out of the way he could see the receptionist's 'important' game of solitaire that obviously kept her busy.

All Morton had to do for the time being was to wait and hope that the ice would have the desired effect. He pondered on what their next move would be if Paul showed signs of reacting favourably to the treatment.

XVI

Post How

During the time that Morton and Katei were waiting for Paul Barton to respond to the drug, they took turns listening in to the conversations that were held within earshot of the fridge that the bag of ice was in. Morton had tried to establish a connection to listen in to mobile phone conversations using several different Government taps, but was only able to access details about the routing of the calls and the raw analogue data. He wondered how GCHQ did their monitoring of speech, if indeed they could. As far as he could tell it would require a physical alteration of the system, instead of the software modifications that he could do.

Morton had as an afterthought added the bugging device to the ornate packaging of the ice, and was now glad that they did. Along with Katei he was gradually building up a picture of what was happening. As far as they could tell, Paul Barton had been lured into aiding an ultra right-wing organisation from the USA This organisation were annoyed by, and worried that the UK did not appear to be taking the war that the US had against terrorism seriously enough. Some of the people involved had positions in the secret security services, who were annoyed at the fact that the US had withdrawn from its overseas detention centres. They bemoaned that fact that their 'prisoners' had to be treated 'fairly'.

From what they could piece together, this group had infiltrated a terrorist ring in the UK, and were supplying it with classified information that the UK had shared with the US. They understood that some sort of massive co-ordinated terrorist attack was to take place, but not how or when. The object of instigating the attack was to make the UK government sit up and take notice of the possibility of further attacks. The code words that they kept hearing were Tornado, Typhoon, and Tsunami, in connection with Autumn Storm. Morton mused that it might have something to do with RAF aircraft.

In any case they had decided that Morton's plan was sound. They would have to get Paul Barton away, determine what plans the terrorist group had, and then alert the security services. Katei had been all for alerting someone else straight away, but Morton wanted time to get his erstwhile friend sorted out.

As the days wore on Katei and Morton started to get the feeling that Paul Barton was reacting to the treatment. They decided to try using Katei's manipulation of phone signals again, to get a feel for what was happing in the office where Paul Barton was speaking. The connection lasted for about five minutes, and then stopped. "Whoops," said Katei, "I think someone knows that we are looking at them. The way that they stopped talking and left the room, might just mean that they are on to us."

They made their way up to the ground floor, and Katei made some tea, while they tried to gather their thoughts.

Morton was just biting into a Rich Tea biscuit when there was a massive bang at the front door. They both looked up at the CCTV that had been set up at the entrance along with Katei's gravity mantrap. Katei could not help but laugh, even though the situation was quite serious. There were several men in the entrance hallway all floating about unable to escape, and occasionally gently bumping into each other. As they watched the only man not in the trap tried to rescue one of his compatriots, and became trapped as well.

"I think that's all of them," said Katei. "All of them?" queried Morton. "Yes," replied Katei, "all of the ones that we have seen so far. There may be more, but those are the only ones we have ever seen with Barton. It probably means that Barton is now alone. I suggest that if we are going to rescue him then now is the time."

They had already made plans for the rescue, and it only took a few minutes to gather the required things together, and for them to exit into a courtyard out the back. From there they went out through a small corridor that provided the back of the surrounding buildings with a fire exit.

"How long before they are able to get help and be rescued? Do you think?" asked Morton. Katei was of the opinion that they would be found within half an hour, and it would take a similar time to get the electricity to the building turned off.

XVII

Post Haste

They arrived at the offices that Paul Barton was in, as swiftly as they could. They were lucky in that they were able to hail a taxi fairly quickly. Morton nodded at the receptionist who was still 'busy', and they made their way to the lift. The lift took an interminable time to reach the top floor. They searched through several rooms there, eventually finding Paul Barton locked in a room full of charts.

Paul Barton looked up amazed. Barton was not normally short of words, but on this occasion he was utterly stumped. Morton broke the silence by saying "Good Morning Paul, how are you feeling?" "Good." said Barton "very, very good – but how?" Katei cleared her throat and spoke. "You have a brain tumour," she said bluntly. "We smuggled in a drug to reduce the size of it." She went on to explain to Paul Barton how they had dosed his ice.

"I don't know where to start," said Barton, "perhaps I should start with the pain and the voices. The voices told me that I had a special job to do, and that I would be the chosen one. I would know I was doing right, because the pain would stop. I realise now that I was going demented." He paused and walked around looking at the walls. "This!" he squeaked. "How can we stop this?" He gestured to the maps and diagrams on the wall, and then went on speaking "There are so many people involved. I have been arguing with them during the past two days that the project is insane. I think they guessed that I was no longer insane myself, which is why I was locked up in here."

Morton and Katei recounted events, from Katei discovering Morton in the Pod up until the present. "Sorry," said Barton banging his head. "I am so sorry, and I nearly killed you. The voices in my head said that you would be useful later, but this lot wanted you dead. I told this lot that you were dead. I suppose that they thought that you would recognise something wrong with me and take some sort of action." "Well," said Morton, "we have taken action, but who are 'this lot'?" "Project Team Tsunami they call themselves," replied Barton. Paul Barton led them around maps on the walls. He explained how the team wanted to take advantage of the wet weather that the UK had every autumn. The plan was to cut off certain parts of the grid and cause a power loss to the London Underground. The effect would be that with the wet weather, the tube would start to flood. Barton showed them a graph of Victoria Tube Station. "Normally," he said, "eight gallons are pumped out every second to stop the thing flooding. In the weather we have been having recently it will be even more." Barton explained that there would be a point of no return. A point at which the pumps would not, when switched on again, be able to remove the water.

"Are there not back-up plans though?" asked Katei. Barton replied, "Yes, but only very limited now. There used to be several power stations within London that could take over and provide power. Local Government, and privatised companies have gradually pared the back-up to the bone. Where they aim to hit the National Grid with explosives it will take a long time to re-route power to the system. And there is more." Morton raised his eyebrows. Barton went on speaking, saying, "There are plans to hold up water further up the Thames. Some of it is already happening anyway. People in Maidenhead, up the Thames in bloody bucolic Berkshire are already complaining that the bypass Jubilee River is too full. There are personnel standing by to open sluice gates in a coordinated fashion to cause the biggest possible surge. And there is still more." This time it was the turn of Katei to raise an eyebrow in a query. Barton continued. "This is the trickiest part of the operation because the Thames Barrier is fairy well protected from attack. The plan here is to co-ordinate the surge in the river with the outgoing tide. Once Project Team Tsunami have taken over, the Barrier will be raised. The combination of outflow and surge will hit the barrier causing a huge rebound of water that will exacerbate the flooding problem.

Katei asked how the barrier could be raised if much of London's power was cut off. Barton explained that the Barrier had a back-up generator that could be used in emergencies, and the team would utilise that.

Morton suddenly realised that while they had been talking a lot of time had passed by. They had to leave the building quickly. Morton asked Paul for the swiftest way to leave the building. Paul pointed toward the fire escape door. "But we are at the top of the building," protested Morton, "it would take ages to run down the stairs." Paul went over to the door and opened it. "We just jump down there," he said. Morton found himself looking into a tube that went down to the next floor. Paul explained that it was one of the latest inventions of the foundation. A tube runs from top to bottom of the building with flaps at each of the floors. In each of the fire escape rooms there are kept polystyrene 'life' rings with a rubber and composite inner. This is placed around the chest, with the user holding their arms over their head. The user jumps in the hole, and once the system is activated descent is controlled by air pressure. The system is designed to work normally with a computer, but should still work if the computer is inactive. Paul warned that the polystyrene gets very hot on the way down, as it contacts the tube all the way round.

The three of them having donned the rings jumped down the hole in the prescribed sequence, but not without some trepidation. Morton was the first to arrive fairly heavily on the ground floor, and he scurried out of the way to allow Katei to follow him. As he moved out of the tube he heard the flap of the floor above go pop as it let Katei through.

They peered out through the fire escape doors making sure that the coast was clear. They made their way out of the building slowly, so as not to draw attention to themselves. They moved quicker once they had cleared the immediate vicinity of the building. As they hurried down the road, Morton spotted the same large MPV that the ruffians had arrived in at his house. No one in the MPV seemed to have noticed them. Once the vehicle was out of the way they ran to the point that Katei and Morton had examined several weeks earlier. The key that Morton had purchased opened the door with ease.

They were nearly blown off their feet by the draught that came out of the door. Paul and Katei stepped in and walked down the narrow flight of steps inside. Morton locked the door behind him and followed them. After the narrow flight of steps there was a large spiral staircase, of a type once common in the Underground. About two thirds of the way down Morton waved at the others to be quiet. They passed a door that was obviously reasonably new. "I don't think anyone is using it," said Morton, "but just to be careful."

At the bottom of the stairway they found themselves in a tunnel slightly larger than the standard Underground, but with the standard cream and purple tiling much covered in dust. They then passed several corridors with painted signs like 'Enquiries & Committee Room', refer-ences to the committee rooms used during the early 20th Century War. They could hear the noise of passing tube trains as they proceeded. Further on they passed though some ancient switching equipment painted uniformly in grey. They made their way though some more passage-ways eventually ending up at a platform, albeit a very short one.

During the escape Paul Barton had been endeavouring to collect his thoughts. He tried to remember what it was like when he had the voices in his head. His ears, (or was it his brain?) still strained to hear what the voices might command next. In a way he still felt reliant on them. He felt devoid of self-direction. The descent into the Underground, with its attendant associations to the war that his grandfather had told him tales about, brought back memories he thought he had lost long ago. At his grandfather's knee he had heard stories of great heroism, and also of terrible sadness. He recalled being confused that his grandfather placed such value on the UK defence forces, but so vehemently hated war.

Standing on the platform, Paul could hear thumps and scuffling sounds coming from directions where he felt noises should not be coming from. He fancied he could hear a baby cry, and then a woman scream. He thought perhaps he could hear laughter in the distance. His brain preyed on the words man's laughter and manslaughter. Paul physically shook himself to dispel the ghosts of the past century. He was delighted that his greatest friend Morton had rescued him, but anxious about what he had done, and confused about his own inner-being. His mind then wandered around the word 'id' and the constant need for ID. Was the modern world what his grandfather had fought for?

Paul's reverie was broken by a voice close to him. A voice that was insistent and querying, but polite. "Do we just hail a train then?" asked Katei. "Something like that!" said Morton. "I don't know how much of the rest of the complex is in use, but higher authority insisted that this here red button remained." On saying that Morton pressed the button. He then motioned for them to move back in the corridor.

Within a few minutes a tube train arrived, and the set of doors adjacent to the small platform opened. Some people sitting in the carriage looked up mildly surprised to see other people getting on in the middle of nowhere. A couple of individuals rustled their papers and went back to reading. A group of teenagers carried on with their conversations, shouting to make everyone else hear over their personal stereo earplugs.

The three made their way via Kings Cross to Paddington, where Morton booked them on the train to the West Country. He had some trouble with the booking because the ticket clerk insisted that if Morton was paying with cash then he needed to see the ID cards of all three travellers. After Morton returned from his ordeal he asked Katei how it was that things were so bad that you could not move about without an ID card. "Don't worry," said Katei, "it's just petty bureaucrats making rules for themselves, and they get away with it a lot of the time.

XVIII

To the West

Morton had not been able to book seats on the train. The booking clerk told him that he should have booked a lot earlier if he wanted a seat. "People are always complaining about this," Morton was told. When he asked if that was so, why did the company not put more carriages on, he was told that too often the train ran with empty seats. This is why Morton and his company were walking up the platform peering into the train. The back end of the train was packed with people standing, and with people in the corridor alongside. At the front of the train there were three totally empty carriages. Unsure as to whether these had been booked or not they thought they would sit here anyway, and be prepared to move if someone arrived who had booked a seat.

No one had appeared to take their seats by the time the train had started so they stayed where they were. Sometime later a scruffy man in a scruffy uniform came down the train to check their tickets. They held the tickets out, and the official duly scanned them. Having verified their tickets he said, "And now your official ID." "Please!" said Katei. "What?" asked the official. Katei said, "You could say please." "Never mind that bollocks," said the man. "Either you got official ID or you ain't, and you go back there." He said this jerking his thumb toward the back of the train.

"What's this all about?" asked Morton. The official looked at him balefully and said, "Government in' it? Loads of the government civil service have been moved to the South West 'cause it's cheaper. So these carriages are booked out to them at all times so that they can easily get back to meetings in London. They don't want anyone messing their seats up like." Morton reached inside his jacket and found his wallet. He was about to extract his Mr Tracy ID, but before he could do so Paul Barton whipped out his own ID. The inspector harrumphed, and pointed his scanner at it. "OK sir," he said, "looks like you are entitled to stay here with guests. I'll be back later with refreshments."

Morton returned his card and wallet to his jacket, and then reached in the other side to get out a map. "Here," he said as he pointed to a mark on the map, "is the facility." Paul asked him how he proposed to be let off the train at the point he wanted, bearing in mind that the route they were on was not fully covered by shuttle trains due to long tunnels on the route. Morton replied, "Exactly, and skulduggery!" Katei said, "Well we have been lucky so far, but I don't quite understand what the two of you are discussing." Morton pointed to the map again, and launched into an explanation. "Here is the middle of a hill. This hill has the railway line passing through it. Now in the war at the beginning of the last century ammunition trains would enter the tunnel in the guise of ordinary transport. Right in the middle of the tunnel is a set of points that take you into a siding that takes you off to an ammunition warehouse. In the war another identical train would be already waiting there to come steaming out as though it were the same train passing through the tunnel."

Katei nodded and said, "But what is that to us?" Morton replied that the site had progressed since then, and was now used for other functions as well. He went on, "There used to be a whole load of secure communication stuff in there, but they had to move it all up to the surface when civilian staff took over. Never mind bomb proof and electromagnetic radiation proof, staff cannot be allowed to work underground anymore. Health and safety you know. But we should be able to find all that we need in the old store rooms."

"Anyway," said Morton, flicking the corner of the map around Katei's ear, "back to what I was saying. As I understand it these trains have special interlocks with the doors so that if a door is open the train will not move. We could try pulling the communication cord, but I suspect that the driver, or automatic system has been instructed not to stop in a tunnel. So what we need is a key. Now that pompous little man we saw earlier has just such a key sticking out of the bunch he has on his waist. He has them all on show, no doubt, to show us just how officious and important he is. It's the yellow 'plasticky' key. Now let's try and get a plan together."

The officious official eventually arrived with a trolley containing some quite reasonable looking food and some drinks. Morton pointed to a bottle of premixed gin and tonic, and asked the man for it. "ID sir?" said the man. "ID?" asked Morton full knowing what the answer would be. "Your ID sir," the official said, "I need to check your drink allowance." He scanned Morton's ID. He then ran an intoximeter past Morton's lips. Morton had just wet his lips with some brandy from a hip flask. "NO sir," said the official, you are already indicating over your limit." Morton stood up, towering over the official who was bent over the trolley, and shouted, "WHAT!" The little official cringed in front of him. "It's more than my job's worth," he said. "Dismissal and a huge fine." Katei then stood up and held on to the man. "Oh dear!" she said, "my colleague is just a bit cross, perhaps you could return later?" She said this as she put a comforting arm around the man. Unbeknown to him she was holding out the pink key so that Paul could snip it off the elastic string, which is what he did.

The rest was easy. Morton had been gauging the speed of the train, and at the appropriate time after entering the tunnel he reached out of the door window carefully and inserted the key in the door lock. There was an immediate jolt as the brakes automatically cut in, and this was followed by a metallic screeching, as some of the wheels locked up. The three of them clambered down from the train with their equipment, and with some difficulty. Morton had more difficulty getting the door to slam shut again. They quickly ran back down the track to where they hoped the siding was. It was not at all easy to tell where it was in the dark.

Paul who was at the front of the group eventually spotted it, as there was a dim light from the far end of the siding. This dim light became a lot brighter as they finally reached some ancient platforms. They walked up the ramp end of one of the platforms and then along the platform to where there was a place where they could sit. As Paul and Morton got their breath back, Katei was examining the concrete platform. She got down on her hands and knees and traced a crescent in the concrete. There were a lot of these marks in the platform. Katei queried Paul and Morton as to what they might be. Morton asked Katei if she had ever seen an artillery shell. Katei said that she had seen some in a museum that were huge and looked like enormous rifle bullets. Morton said that was just what she was looking at; the imprint of a shell that had been dropped. Katei looked puzzled for a moment and then said, "Ah well I suppose they would not have had the primer loaded." Katei sat down again, and tried to imagine the place full of people unloading, or loading up ammunition. Paul Barton held his forehead, as the ghosts of the past seemed to be whispering in his ears. He tried hard not to imagine the past.

XIX

In the West

When they had all got their breath back they walked off the platform and down a tunnel at the back. As they walked along strip lights flickered on, lighting the way. Katei peered into huge storage caverns either side, marvelling at the work of the Royal Engineers in creating this place. Eventually they came to a cavern with a large door, and a small door inset into it.

They entered the room though the small door. Morton scrabbled about for a moment or two trying to ascertain where the lights were operated. So far all the lights had operated automatically as they approached. Eventually he found how to activate them, and what was obviously an entrance hall was illuminated. The hallway had several doors leading off. Each door had a description on it. Katei just had a chance to read that one of the doors led to a laboratory, and that another led to an exercise room. Morton led them though a door marked 'Accommodation'.

The accommodation consisted of a large living room, a reasonably sized, and stocked kitchen, and several bedrooms. At this point they all realised just how tired they were. Paul suggested that he would investigate the kitchen while Katei and Morton put their feet up for a bit. First Paul brought through some coffee, and then a collection of nibbles. Katei wondered if perhaps Paul was not quite as bad as she first imagined. When she looked at his face, it looked different to when she had seen him at the Foundation. She wondered if it was the brain tumour, or some side effect of it, that had previously subtly altered his facial features.

Paul caught Katei looking at him, and she looked away embarrassed. Katei got up and collected together the utensils that they had been using to eat the small, but adequate feast. "I'll take these out to the kitchen, and see what else is in there," she said as she busied herself with the job.

While Katei was out in the kitchen, Paul stretched out in the chair, and looked over at Morton. "Very nice lady! How did you hook up with her?" asked Paul. Morton and Paul talked for some time about how they had arrived at their current situation. During the conversation Paul kept apologising to Morton for his previous bad behaviour. And it was finally on this subject that they realised there was a problem. The drug that Paul had unknowingly taken had of course had the desired effect, but they now had none left to administer to Paul.

Morton knew that there was a small laboratory available, but he was not sure what could be done for Paul. When Katei returned from the kitchen, the two men were hunched over a laptop. Katei peered over their shoulders to see that they were accessing information on tumours and treatments. The most common treatment for a tumour appeared to be counter attack with a designer virus.

Morton suggested that they had been active enough for one day, and that he for one needed to get some sleep. He explained how the site had been set up with a variety of accommodation areas, and laboratories. He was not sure how much of it was still maintained if the country was now on a low terrorist alert. Certainly in his, now not so, recent memory lots of money had been spent on it.

The following morning found the three of them in the laboratory. Here they were able to perform a non-invasive scan of Paul's head, and were able to run the results through a computer program designed for the purpose. The program produced a series of intermediate results, and then prompted for a blood analysis. This was also a painless process, as there was a machine designed specifically for the purpose.

Morton watched the program as it gave status displays as it worked though the possibilities. Katei watched Morton as he frowned more and more at the screen. He turned to see her watching him. "Not good," he said, and motioned Kati to come over. "The trouble is that to prepare the virus that we need could take several months. The tumour however is liable to grow a lot quicker than that. I am not a surgeon, but given the location of the thing, I think it would be nigh on impossible to remove it. It might be possible to shrink it some more with the drug treatment, but it looks like the treatment might become ineffective too."

Katei looked at the final results. The tumour, now that it was able to start growing again, would soon be putting pressure back onto Paul's brain. His headaches and 'voices' might soon return. Up until now Paul had hovered at a distance, but when he heard the dismay in their voices he came closer. Morton showed him through the results.

After a long silence, Morton broke in saying, "We have to get you to a proper medical establishment." Paul shook his head. "No," he said, "much to dangerous. I am not sure what my colleagues in crime have made of me for last few weeks as I recovered. I got into some strange arguments. It may be that the tumour will not get me, but they will."

Morton paced around for a while. "OK" he said, "we can do some more research, but we also need to plan how we can let the appropriate intelligence people know what is going on. We need to get you out of all of this somehow.

The days dragged out, as they trawled through knowledge bases for alternative treatments. Morton racked his brains trying to work out how he could contact someone in the intelligence services to let them know of the proposed attack. They watched news bulletins that further depressed them with reports of more wet weather, and some localised flooding. Morton was worried that an attack could come sooner rather than later. Paul had said that his group were prepared to wait for the ideal circumstances, but he was worried that they were now building up to them.

Morton and Paul worked together to reproduce some of the data that Paul's sect would have been using. To do this they had to gain access to some sensitive computers.

Even though the Weather Forecast data was not in any way secret, some of the network was. The results of the investigation only served to depress Morton and Paul even further. It was forecast that the wet summer was to be followed by an even wetter autumn and winter.

Morton was worried about Paul. He was beginning to look more haggard, and had had some strange outbursts. He had told Katei to go and get in the kitchen, "That is where women should be." Katei, who was also worried about Paul, had immediately absented herself from the room. When Morton had gently remonstrated with Paul, Paul had said, "I can't understand why you're not giving that bit of skirt one. She fancies you like mad you know? Very nice bit of skirt!" Morton red-faced had said that he "did not know", and was left feeling rather confused at the unusual tone of his usually well-behaved friend.

XX

A Bit Wet

Morton and Katei were looking over some hard copy printouts of maps of the UK. The maps contained data on the current weather, and the locations of the military communications stations. Morton had been rotating around different access points to avoid being caught at any one point. It was early morning, and Paul had not as yet arisen.

Morton was just sipping some tea, when Paul came bursting out of his room. "I want out!" he shouted. "You can't keep me prisoner anymore." Morton tried to calm him down. "No," said Paul Barton, "I am calling for help." It was then that Morton realised that Paul had his mobile telephone in his hand. Morton knocked Paul's hand and caused him to lose his grip on the phone. He shouted to Katei to pick it up and turn it off.

Paul held his head and sat down. "I'm so sorry," he sobbed, "but it's all coming back. Headache, voices, the lot." Katei and Morton looked across at each other. They had a plan but it was risky and they had to communicate this to Paul Barton. Barton was in no real state to object to anything and they were not sure if he understood what the trephine device was.

Morton was going to use the ancient form of surgery, albeit with a modern bit of equipment, to make a hole in Paul Barton's head to relieve the build up of pressure. Katei fetched the necessary bits and pieces and Morton decided that the living room was as good a place as anywhere to perform the operation.

It was with some trepidation that Morton put the device in position, and then activated it. The device used electronics, and a gyroscopic action to keep itself located, but was of necessity quite mechanical. There was a small pop, followed by a gurgle, and some blood poured down Paul Barton's face.

What made them jump even more was a gigantic crash as the door was flung open, and several heavily armed uniformed personnel entered. A small man in plain clothes followed them in. "Gotcha," said the little man, "you thought it was clever hiding right under our noses. Well we are a lot cleverer than you. And we know all about your game. Looks like we were just in time before you did that poor fellow in for good." The little man turned around to one of the uniforms and ordered him to fetch first aid.

"Joe Turner," the little man said by way of introduction. He thought for a moment, and then carried on, "and some uniforms, to keep you evil people in order." He walked around the living room looking at the maps. "I can see that we have stopped your little plan in the nick of time. We have had our people watching you since you started hacking into our networks. Buying that key from one of our agents was a big mistake as well, we had you well covered with cameras there."

Morton had been looking on aghast. "But it can all be explained," he started to say. Joe cut him short with a shout of "Quiet!" Looking around and then feeling satisfied with the result he carried on. "We know," he said, "Autumn Storm. A cosy little name for something quite nasty. You lot were planning a Denial Of Service attack on our networks. Our lads are out there even now tracking down the thousands of home computers that you have infected, and putting them right. An interesting operation that might have flooded some very sensitive networks with rubbish data. And we have captured a lot of explosives too. It's just as well that the Prevention of Terrorism Act will let us keep you, in stages, for a year, for some interesting interrogation. I think that you evil pair have lots to tell us."

Again Morton started to splutter his innocence. "But that's only part of it, yes, communications will be disrupted, but that lets the main event take place easier, you have to listen to me, we have to act now. "

"Silence!" shouted Joe. "You, Mr Tracy, and your lady are going to spend time in the detention cell upstairs. You will have several weeks, maybe months to get your story straight. Meanwhile we are going to get this poor chap cleaned up, and arrange for him to be returned home." Joe pointed at two uniforms, and directed them to take hold of Morton and Katei.

They were marched along some corridors, and then upstairs to a large room with what looked like a huge soup kitchen. The walls were painted with several pictures in pastel colours. Joe told them to "Wait." Morton decided that was what they would have to do.

Katei looked about at the place they were in. "A lot of it is from the early twentieth century war," explained Morton. "Some of it has been updated, but a lot of it is out of use. I gather that the pictures were painted using the same paint that aircraft were painted with. I suppose they must have stored it here."

After about twenty minutes Joe arrived back with his contingent of uniforms and arms. "Paul Barton is alive," he said, "no thanks to you. What kind of evil pair are you Tracy people to try and kill a man in such a way? It's just as well that we picked up his mobile phone signal, and acted as quickly as we did." He left again with another command to "Wait!"

After a quarter of an hour Morton started to pace around the large room. He carefully tried the doors around the room, only to find them all locked. He suddenly stopped and patted his pockets. He looked over at Katei. "Pen? Paper?" he asked, and in the asking found what he wanted in his pockets. Katei watched as he wrote out directions. Katei looked at Morton, puzzled. "Why?" she said. "Who wants to go to RAF St Eval?" Morton looked back with a mischievous look in his eyes. "Well," he whispered, "he called us an evil pair so I thought I would leave a fake trail to one of their precious communication stations. An Eval place!"

Katei was even more puzzled now. Morton went over to one of the doors. He put his fingers to his lips and waved to Katei to follow. He took a small combination penknife out of his pocket, and extracted the screwdriver. He then unscrewed the fire alarm. Fire alarm klaxons started to sound. He then put the alarm back together. As soon as the alarm had sounded there had been a 'clunk' sound in the door. "Health and safety" grinned Morton as he opened the door.

They ran along a corridor that was in darkness apart from dim lights illuminating fire exits. They could hear other people in other corridors hurrying along. Eventually they reached a lift. Morton pressed the button and within a few seconds the lift arrived. Morton put his pre-prepared slip of paper in the lift, and sent it up to the surface. He then caught hold of Katei and ran with her back to the room that they had been in and then back down into the depths of the system. They kept on going until they were in what were probably natural caves. Here they slowed up, as it got dark.

"I've never been down this bit," said Morton, but I was told that if I wanted to go to the local pub, then this was the way. But how we are going to do it darkness I don't know." Katei fumbled around in her jacket pocket. "Paul's phone," she said, "it may have a light in it." Morton examined the device it did indeed have a light in it. The phone was a bit on the large side as it was contained in a leather outer case. As Morton extracted the phone from the case to enable the light to function better an ID card dropped out. "Well. Well!" exclaimed Morton, shining the light on the card. It was Morton's ID card that Paul Barton must have kept.

With the aid of the light they were able to reach the end of the cave system. The sight of daylight was welcome to both of them. They cautiously moved forward from the entrance that was indeed close to a pub. In the distance they could hear the sirens of fire engines. They carefully peered over a wall and looked up to the middle of a hill where people were emerging from what was obviously a fire escape. Morton realised that he was picking up body warmth from Katei. The thought passed through his mind that he rather liked that. They then realised that they were in pouring rain, and were getting very cold and wet. Morton had confused thoughts about cuddling up and getting warm, which he banished to the back of his mind.

In the cold, wet, and rather frightened state that they were in, the pub looked like a reasonable option. A very friendly landlord who immediately took them for day-trippers who had got caught in the rain, greeted them. They ordered drinks and sandwiches as they waited for the taxi that the landlord had arranged to arrive.

The taxi took them to the nearest large town, and to the office of a car hire company. Morton hired a car to take them back to London the following morning, feeling relieved that he could now use his own ID. Morton still had some more skulduggery on his mind though. He checked where the nearest express railway station was up line toward London, and headed there. Here they had to wait for the train to arrive from the east, and then consign Paul Barton's phone to the west. Morton left it on a parcel shelf hoping that when found, someone would turn it on and once again send the intelligence services into action. Morton and Katei then retired to an hotel to have a good night's sleep before returning to the capital.

It was not until well past Swindon on the M4 that Morton decided to turn the radio on. The news made them sit up straight. The newsreader was advising people to stay out of London, as there had been a series of power failures. The authorities said that a substation had become overloaded, and on switching power to another station there had been a series of failures. One commentator was quizzing a government minister about housing numbers in the South East, and whether the current boom in population had caused excess stress to the National Grid. "All part of the plan," nodded Morton, "the system was under stress and they knew where to hit it where it hurts."

The minister droned on for a while protesting that it had been down to a previous administration where it had all started to go wrong. An opposition minister denied that any government had caused it and that there obviously needed to be more regulations made for the Power Industry. There were more items about how severe the weather was, and a short item on how a crippling virus was making its way through people's home computers.

Morton had gone white. "It's all happening to plan," he said. "First the destabilisation of the grid, then next a co-ordinated attack by computers connected to broadband Internet to overload the communications network, and stop anyone using remote monitoring to recover the situation."

XXI

Wetter Still

Paul Barton was not having a very good time. He felt that the trephination had put his brain into overdrive. He had been trying to explain to Joe Turner that the man known as Virgil Tracy was not the instigator of all the troubles. He had exacerbated matters by trying to explain about the voices in his head, and how well his brain was functioning now. He imagined that the people he was attempting to talk to must think that the ad hoc operation had sent him totally doolally tap. Especially as his teeth had been chattering with the cold he had suffered.

Paul had also spent a miserable period on the side of a hill outside a fire exit after the evacuation alarm had gone off. Just getting out of the place had tired Paul out, due to the number of corridors he had to walk down, and the steep steps that had to be climbed to the exit. It transpired that the personnel required to check out the installation were located miles away. The local fire service had made some basic checks, but under the supervision of uniformed officers. He'd had to stand in pouring rain with hardly any protection.

Paul had been confined to a bed overnight. He was told that he must rest, and not speak too much. He was very glad of the warmth after getting so chilled in the rain. The medical staff were quite concerned about him, and managed to get Joe Turner to "wait" and be "silent" for a change. Turner fumed silently about this, and for a while set up camp by Paul's bed just in case the medical staff were to leave off for a while. During this time Turner held several conversations with colleagues about the weapons and other equipment that had been seized. Paul had tried to warn Turner that these were just decoys that the intelligence services were expected to find, and therefore give up on locating the really big stashes of murderous munitions, but to no avail.

Joe Turner had left the room some time back, and Paul had just started to nod off, as the strain had started to tell on him. He was brought fully awake again by the door crashing open. Joe Turner was there, red faced and puffing. "What!" he shouted, and then paced around the room, "is the meaning of this?" He was holding the instructions to the communications site that Morton had addressed to Paul. "Are you in on this evil action as well Barton?" Turner stopped snorting, and let his arm hang limp still holding the scrap of paper.

Paul held his hand out for the paper. Turner stiffened up his arm again, and then walked over to Paul holding the paper in both hands so that Paul could read it, but not snatch it away. Paul read the instructions, and then said, "No. I mean yes. No I don't know what I mean. I tried to tell you that it is all my fault." Turner looked at him wearily, he could not work out whether Barton was a victim, or a villain. Paul carried on talking. "But St Eval is in the plan, by causing disruption there it will cause a colossal redirection of communications on to the rest of the backbone networks. But you really need to protect London. I can give you details for that too."

Joe Turner eyed Paul up and down and side to side. "No," he said shaking his head, "I think you are at your imagined devious decoy tricks again. I think you may have a lot to answer for, and I am taking you with me to Cornwall." Paul tried to speak in protest, but Joe Turner yelled "Silence!" and "Wait!" He turned around and started to bark orders to the men in uniform who had dutifully followed him. Paul wondered how such a short man had such a loud voice, and took to commanding people so readily.

Paul's now dry clothes were brought to him; he was then escorted out of the building, and bundled into a waiting car. A uniform sat either side of him, and Joe took command in the passenger seat. As they settled in the car he could hear Joe Turner discussing the whereabouts of the Tracys (aka Morton and Katei). A monitoring station had briefly picked up Barton's mobile phone signal in Exeter. He turned around to Paul and said, "Well, this must be the main event then, we are on the right track. If they turn the phone on again we can nab them. I have arranged for a transport plane to take us to St Mawgan from Bristol Airport, and we then go by Search and Rescue Helicopter to St Eval.

Paul found the journey very rough. The driver drove like a demon with total disregard for the minor roads that they had to navigate. The experience on the main roads was not much better. The aircraft laid on at Bristol was very basic, usually being used for parachute practice. The helicopter ride terrified the wits out of Paul. He felt that if he had not looked a gibbering idiot at the start he now would. He had been perusing a map of Cornwall on the flight, and had spotted a place called Luney Barton near St Austell. He felt that it might be a very apt place for him to go and live.

The old village of St Eval was acquired by compulsory purchase in 1938 and almost completely demolished in order to build an RAF Coastal Command Station. The 13th-century church remains, and stands alone: visible for miles around. It was to this church that Paul was taken. Joe Turner wanted access to the tower, and a body had been sent to find the keys to it. Paul was glad to be somewhere quiet and reasonably warm and dry. As they waited out of the rain, inside, he surveyed the Norman font, and wondered how many had passed under the holy water there.

Joe Turner stamping his foot and cursing broke into Paul's reverie. Turner felt that he had waited long enough for the keys. He was also getting a bit edgy that the backup he had called for to deal with the terrorists had not yet arrived. Turner's plan was to direct operations from the top of the tower. He stomped outside to see the car returning with the woman he had sent to fetch the keys. He grabbed the keys from the woman, and hurried back to the church, leaving the woman flabbergasted, as she had some important information to impart to him. The woman was already feeling uneasy, having been subjected to the same driving as Paul had been. She had also been subjected to a long story about how especially good and quick the driver was. She had felt like asking the over-confident driver if he was good and 'quick' in bed too, as that appeared to be the intent of his dismal chat-up lines.

Paul meekly followed Turner up the tower. He was feeling groggy again. He felt that he could hear the same voices that he had heard in the London Underground. Voices from a past war urging peace in the future. He imagined pilots returning home glad, to see the tower of St Eval Church after some awful mission. Paul suddenly found himself unable to stand, but as luck would have it, the woman from the car had arrived just behind him, and was able to steady him.

Hearing the noise behind, Turner looked around to see what was happening. At the same time there were several loud explosions from the direction of the disused airfield. At this point Paul blacked out, the sound tipping him over the edge. "Sir! Important news!" said the woman as she struggled to let Paul down carefully.

Joe Turner got a grip on himself, and helped the woman with Paul. As they worked the almost dead weight down the stairs the woman explained that the backup would not be happening as a few electricity sub-stations in London had been attacked, and forces were being sent to the capital to be on standby.

As they lay Paul on a pew, he recovered slightly. "The few," he said his brain in a muddle, his mind unable to separate the few that flew in the Battle of Britain, from the few substations that had to be taken out to destabilise the network. The voices were going around in his head like the steady patter of rain on the ground. Joe Turner looked out of the church door to see lights in the rain disappearing in the direction of Mawgan Porth and the coast road. He wondered if his career as a senior intelligence officer was also disappearing down the road.

XXII

Very Wet

The heavy rain meant that restrictions were put on the motorway. The hire car that Morton had was equipped with all the latest safety devices, so that even though he wanted to go faster when the rain eased up a bit he could not, because the car was still reacting to the motorway control beacons. Some cars flashed passed him that were obviously older models. Morton wanted to be back at the Foundation so that he could use the bona-fide links there, and his proper ID to alert the security services to the HQ of the villains so that they could see the plans in their entirety.

It was nearly two hours after Swindon that they got to Slough. As they slowed up with the traffic to pass though the conurbation Morton mused on the poem about friendly bombs and Slough. "Bombs!" said Katei. Morton started "What?" he queried, "can you read my mind?" Katei reached forward and turned the radio up louder to listen to the report. "There are reports of several explosions in London. Some people described the noise as if a bomb had gone off. The authorities say that it is probably a knock-on effect of the earlier problems with the electricity system. It is thought that many people may have to spend the night in London as the whole Underground system has ground to a halt. Several people have had to be rescued from between stations. Engineers are working hard to fix faults and the system should be working again by late this evening."

By now they were nearly at Heathrow. As they approached, the Satnav started to blink with an arrow and then a cross. The M4 was closed into London and they were being diverted onto the M25. "Blast," said Morton, "I think we need a new plan." He glumly followed the traffic off the M4.

They headed around the M25 to the M3, while Katei fiddled with the Satnav to work out which roads were open. As far as they could tell all roads into the capital were electronically cordoned off. Morton's modern hire car would grind to a halt if he tried to ignore the warnings. Katei stopped fiddling with the Satnav, and fished the owner's handbook out of the glove compartment. She flipped through a few pages to the section on fuses. The car fuses were very handily placed under a mat on the front parcel shelf. Katei lifted out the removal tool from its slot, and then selected a fuse. An amber lamp lit on the dashboard and the Satnav went dead.

The car was now free of safety features and Morton was able to head off the Motorway. Once off the motorway, only older cars were moving about. Newer cars were unable to proceed toward London. Having now taken a prolonged route eastwards, Morton's new plan now was to go straight to the Thames Barrier and see what could be done from there, or from the Port of London Authority.

As they approached the Barrier the weather was getting worse. Morton was still uncertain as to what he was actually going to do when he got there. When they did get there he was still not sure. The main gate had been blown apart, and there was a lot of debris in the street. It was difficult to see what was going on, as the rain was so heavy.

Morton recalled that the 'terrorist' sect had been very careful in selecting the right explosives to break into the Barrier. He remembered Barton telling him about the research that had been done by them into the anti-terrorist parts of the establishment.

Morton and Katei got out of the car, and moved toward the barrier gates, office, and the possibility of some shelter from the rain. As they tried to take in the scene, a group of people came up behind them. Morton was a bit wary, as he did not want to be locked up by Joe Turner again.

"Port of London Authority," said a man at the front. "Any idea what is going on?" Morton looked at him and said, "Yes, only too well, but what can you tell me?" The man from the PLA who was called Gordon told Morton that they had heard an explosion. They had phoned the police, but had been told to wait until they arrived. They had then seen the barrier raised, and had heard another explosion. A few minutes later there was yet another explosion, and smoke could be seen coming from the reserve control room on the North Bank.

Morton filled Gordon in on what he knew about the situation, and between them they theorised that the villains must have raised the barriers, and then destroyed both control rooms. By this time they could hear sirens in the distance. A few minutes later several police cars arrived with armoured police. The senior policeman recognised Gordon, and asked him for an update. Several police then made their way into the building.

Within a few minutes the police had ascertained that the villains had struck and left very quickly. One of the policemen had with him a man from the Barrier operations team. The man had obviously suffered during the attack and was barely coherent. He managed to explain that the attack had come very swiftly with a combination of explosions and noxious gas. "They didn't get at the individual override controls," he stated in a halting voice. "If we can get power we can open it".

The lead policeman exclaimed. "If!" "The whole of bloody London is saying that. If we had power." Morton looked mournfully around and then all of a sudden, "Of course!" he exclaimed, "that's it! This place has its own backup generator. That is what Paul explained to us." As he finished speaking the police were escorting more people out of the stricken building. Morton managed to find a man, Peter, who knew about the generator. He went over to the generator with Peter. Morton got one of the other men who had now recovered well to brief the police on the manual operation of the Barrier.

Morton and Peter got the generator up and running in no time. As they checked out the operation and the reconnections they had made Morton became curious about part of the system that seemed redundant. "Oh that!" said Peter. "Yeh, once upon a time we used to run the generator up and sell power into the grid. Dunno why we still don't do that, this thing produces way over what is required for the local operation. It is just like a mini Power Station."

While the police and staff who could work saw to the lowering of the Barrier Morton went in search of the senior police officer. He checked out with him that the situation in the Underground was serious, much more serious than had been admitted on the radio. The officer found him one of the senior electrical engineers to talk to on the phone. Morton quickly explained about the massive generator that the Barrier had. The engineer could hardly believe his ears. "Of course!" he said, "I had forgotten all about that! It's the only source of power left in London. We have already created dedicated circuits to ring fence the Underground for when we get power back, but our sources from the north keep tripping out with other loads from new housing conurbations that we can't detach from the system. A source in the near south would be ideal."

It took a little while to restore the Barrier before they wanted to cut the power fully over to the grid. When the cutover was made the strain on the generator was quite apparent. Morton again spoke to the electrical engineer to make sure that the power was being only used to keep the pumps going. The engineer assured him that as far as he knew it was. He also thanked Morton for saving his reputation, and London.

XXIII

Drying Out

Morton and Katei managed to make a quiet exit from the Thames Barrier. As news came in that the most vulnerable central and southern portions of the London Underground were safe there was much backslapping and shaking of hands going on. They slowly retreated to the hire car. Morton did stop to talk to the senior police officer again. He was rather hoping that the man would be able to converse with the other services, and explain what had happened. He was also anxious that the trouble at his house could be cleared up.

It took several weeks for the dust to settle, and for people to be found to take the blame for some aspects, and others to take the glory. Morton attempted as much as possible to stay out of the limelight, and let various actions take their course. Until things had calmed down, Morton and Katei stayed in rooms at the Foundation.

It was at the Foundation where they met Paul Barton again. Morton had arranged for him to be brought there with an escort. The hole in Paul Barton's head had provided him relief for a short while, and Katei had arranged for more drugs to be supplied to help reduce the growth of the tumour. Morton and Katei had drawn on the expertise of some of the top doctors to find a suitable course of action.

What Morton had not expected was Joe Turner and some plain clothes escorts. When Joe saw Morton his jaw dropped open. "Who?" he shouted, just like he was shouting one of his "Wait!" commands. "I was told I was to see a Mr Morton Elise and a lady called Miss Cooksie. What the bloody heck are the Tracys doing here?" Morton drew out his ID card and held it up next to his face, so that Joe could see the two together. "A case of mistaken Identity?" he laughed. He said this as he realised that the uniformed police officer accompanying the group was the one that attended the Thames Barrier.

"Sorry sir," said the policeman, "I have tried to explain the situation properly to Mr Turner several times, but he is always preoccupied with some other matter and keeps telling me to wait." Morton nodded, "Yes, don't we know!"

An additional hour or so was taken up with more formalities, before the large group were led by Morton to the controlled substances storage area, where he had arranged for them to all gain entrance. Morton had spent some time refitting a number of the machines, and had commissioned software upgrades or new hardware for the faulting computers.

The doctors had meanwhile found a slightly quicker way to engineer a virus to attack Paul Barton's tumour, but it would still be a touch and go business. Morton's suggestion that Paul Barton had taken up once he became lucid again was for Paul to be placed in suspension until a cure could be synthesised. Morton felt uneasy about this. He felt it was a bit like looking at the last page or two of a book to see what the ending was, and then realising that there was a lot more to the story.

They helped Barton into the chamber, and assisted him to become comfortable. Morton checked that Barton's fingers would reach the emergency flush button. Morton pressed the appropriate button, and the lid to the capsule started to close. As Barton took on a green tinge the lid gently made its way down, a red flashing indicator on its side.

The others left the room apart from Katei. Morton slumped into a chair, and flopped across a table. Katei could see that he was totally exhausted. She pulled up a chair next to Morton and put her arm around him. "I'm so sorry," she said, "I think I have come to understand the bond of friendship between you and Paul. It will be alright I am sure." Morton lifted his head up and nodded. "Yes, hopefully he will be in there for a lot shorter time than I was."

As Morton sat there he remembered how pleasant it had been to feel Katei's warmth against him as they watched the evacuation of the caves after Morton's use of the alarm. He held on to Katei's arm, and pulled himself around to look at her properly. "I'm sorry," she said, "I didn't mean to be grinning but it's just that Paul did remind me of a frog, and now there he is looking like one." Morton grinned back, "You know," he said, "that tumour thing is not all bad." Katei looked into Morton's eyes. "Yes," murmured Morton, "as Paul pointed out, when he was affected by it: a very nice bit of skirt".